The Limner's Daughter

Also by Mary Stetson Clarke

Petticoat Rebel
The Iron Peacock

The
Limner's Daughter

by Mary Stetson Clarke

The Viking Press   *New York*

First published in 1967 by The Viking Press, Inc.
625 Madison Avenue, New York, N.Y. 10022

Published simultaneously in Canada by
The Macmillan Company of Canada Limited

Library of Congress catalog card number: AC 67-10649

Fic 1. American history
2. Massachusetts
3. Canals

Printed in U.S.A. by The Book Press Incorporated

For my children, Stetson, Susan, and Joyce

Contents

	Foreword	9
1	Aboard the Packet	11
2	Across the Mudflats	21
3	The Marsh Cottage	28
4	The Stagecoach	39
5	An Accident	48
6	Decayed Gentlewomen	58
7	The Spinning Loft	71
8	Two Letters	79
9	The Search	88
10	On the Middlesex Canal	94
11	The Vine-covered Door	107
12	The Lyte Homestead	111
13	The Bible Box	117
14	The Secret of the Vine-covered Door	124
15	"His father's a Tory!"	133

Contents

16   Not Worth a Continental   138

17   A Second Offer   143

18   Ghosts of Old Indian Fires   148

19   The Rowan Tree Inn   157

20   Beside the Towpath   165

21   The First Guest   170

22   An Invitation   176

23   Soirée for a Countess   184

24   The Mob   192

25   A Warrant for Arson   199

26   "God send you a good deliverance!"   207

27   The Verdict   230

28   A New Life   240

     Acknowledgments   253

Foreword

Although the principal characters in this story are imaginary, many were personages who left their mark upon the early years of this country's independence—Loammi Baldwin, his son Loammi II, Sally Thompson, the Countess of Rumford, Mrs. Deborah Snow, Mrs. Jephthah Richardson, James Sullivan, Theophilus Parsons, Theodore Sedgwick, Samuel Sewall, and Isaac Parker. Occasional reference is made to the brilliant scientist Benjamin Thompson, Count Rumford, famed for his research in physics. Only his relationship to Darius Lyte is fictitious; other incidents in which he figures are a part of history.

Much of the action is set against the background of the Middlesex Canal, the first canal in the United States, which was begun in 1793, opened in 1803, and operated until 1860 between Boston and Lowell.

In Woburn, Massachusetts, near a remnant of the canal and in front of his family home, one of the most elegant mansions of its day, stands a statue of Loammi Baldwin, sturdy citizen who served the youthful United States as

Revolutionary War Colonel, Special Justice, legislator, First Sheriff of Middlesex County, selectman, chief constructor and Superintendent of the Middlesex Canal, and disseminator of the Baldwin apple, who said he "would wish to apply the last day of his labors to planning and executing a canal, and planting out an orchard or something that would result in permanent benefit to posterity."

Loammi Baldwin II was also born and brought up in the Baldwin mansion. Known as the Father of Civil Engineering in the United States, he built his life and career upon the belief that "a man's ability is a debt he owes to the welfare of his fellow men."

1

Aboard the Packet

It was all far too good to be true, she thought, pushing back her chip bonnet and letting the afternoon sun shine full upon her face. This couldn't be Amity Lyte, the schoolroom drudge, here on the deck of the packet *Rover,* sailing up Long Island Sound to Boston this fifteenth day of June in 1805. Three days ago she had been trapped in a stuffy classroom at Miss Reed's school in New York correcting French compositions. Today she had no duty more onerous than watching her brother Timothy as he dangled a fishline over the sloop's rail.

She took a deep breath of the tangy air. What glorious weather! To think that the teachers had warned her of storms and seasickness, pressing upon her smelling salts and vials of malodorous remedies. Of them all, only Mlle. Cécile Armand, the French mistress, had suggested that the voyage might be less than intolerable.

"Every journey can be an adventure, *chérie*," she had said with a smile, and to prepare Amity for it she had sat up night after night to make her a new frock. She had set each stitch with a quick push of her gold thimble, and she had bitten off each thread with a sharp click of her teeth almost as if she were biting off the head of a father who cared so little for his daughter that he'd not provide suitable clothing for her.

Amity leaned against the rail, tall and slim in the new high-waisted gown, her body swaying with the ship's gentle motion. She had coiled her tawny hair high on her head as was proper for a young woman of sixteen, though she wished she had dared to crop it short in the latest French fashion. Her face was longer than oval, with sensitive lips, a narrow nose, and wide-set gray eyes that even in the sunlight seemed clouded by inward shadows.

The dark-haired six-year-old beside her tilted his anxious face upward, his mouth a tremulous curve. "Do you think I'll really catch a fish?" he asked.

How long since Tim had truly smiled? Or laughed? Amity felt the familiar stab of pain. Deliberately she forced her thoughts away from the dark corner of her mind and put an arm about Tim's shoulders. "Indeed I do! I think you'll catch a great big one!" she said, giving him a quick hug.

Mercy, how thin he was! If only she could see to his meals, make sure that he had proper nourishing food. There was a chance she might soon. Determinedly she checked herself. Better not to hope. Better to accept each day as it came. Who could tell what new trouble tomorrow might bring?

"What will happen to the fish if I catch one?" asked Tim uncertainly.

"The cook will fix it for your supper," boomed a hearty voice. Captain Abbot, his round red face creased in a smile, halted in his leisurely pacing of the deck. "Nothing like a fresh piece of fish, I always say. See that you catch a big one." He laid a freckled hand on the boy's hair, ruffled it with a friendly gesture, then went on his way.

What an easy way some men had with children! If only Father—

Almost as if Tim were reading her thoughts, he said, "Do you think Father will be cross, Amity?"

Surely there was nothing wrong about fishing. The steward had volunteered the line and a bit of salt pork for bait, saying with a wink that Tim was big enough to work for his passage. But who could tell how Father would feel, or what he would say? For three years Darius Lyte had been so shut within himself that no one knew what he was thinking. His face was like a mask; he rarely spoke. He seemed a ghost of the warm, loving parent of long ago.

"I don't think Father cares," said Amity, choosing each word with bitter precision.

"Should I go down and ask him?" Tim asked, his dark eyes troubled.

The poor child had been so ordered about in the house where he'd been boarded that he hardly dared take a step without asking permission. "You'd better not disturb him; he's probably asleep."

She couldn't bear to see Tim disappointed, and Father might take it into his head to forbid this harmless diversion, just as he had forbidden her to speak to the only other passenger aboard the *Rover*. It had not been easy to ignore Mr. Samuel Baldwin these two days past. It was not easy at this minute, as he leaned against the rail some ten feet away, though he kept his gaze carefully on the Connecticut shoreline.

A few years older than she, he was more wholesome than handsome, with vitality in his roughhewn features. He hardly looked the type to lead young girls astray. The twinkle in his eyes seemed more witty than wicked, and his manner had been courteous and straightforward from the moment he had come aboard in New York.

Amity had been standing on deck with her father and Tim, and could not help overhearing the newcomer's request that the captain delay sailing until Colonel Loammi Baldwin's consignment of books could be brought aboard. Just then Darius Lyte had clapped one hand across his eyes, muttered that he had a blinding headache, and stumbled to his cabin. And there he had remained, though how he had endured the stuffy little cubicle for two whole days she couldn't imagine.

Amity clenched her hands, fighting away the fear that besieged her. Was her father's ailment a passing indisposition brought on by intensive use of his eyes these past few weeks when he helped his pupils finish their calligraphy exhibits for the school's final exhibition? Or was it a recurrence of that other terrifying illness when he had withdrawn so far into his private grief that no one, not even his own son and daughter, had been able to reach him?

Her mind shied away from the memory. He was better now, thanks to the friend who had found him a position teaching the art of fine handwriting at Miss Reed's school. And he would continue to improve when teaching at Mrs. Snow's school in Boston. He must, she told herself. But still the fear persisted.

"There's an old lady lives near us," Sam went on, "who won't let any cats near her place for fear they'll hurt the birds. She gets all riled up about those cats, but she won't throw a stone or a stick at them, no, sir. She just claps her hands or shakes her apron."

Tim lifted his head, a trace of a smile on his tear-streaked face. "She sounds nice," he said gravely.

For a few minutes the three stood in silence. Small waves slapped against the *Rover*'s hull. Sunlight glinted on the water like a thousand mirrors tilting. A steady breeze blew with refreshing coolness.

Suddenly there was a commotion at the door of the galley—a loud shout, and the sound of running feet. The cook darted out, waving an iron spoon, and bellowing, "Fire! Fire!"

Sailors appeared from nowhere, rushing across the deck. The captain sprinted for the galley. "Where is it?" he bawled.

"In the hold," yelled the cook. He pointed with the spoon at smoke coming up through cracks in a corner of the cookhouse.

In seconds the captain dashed out of the galley, his face redder than ever. He shot orders at the crew. "Josh, you and Ben lift off that hatch cover. And take care. It could blow like a cannon. Jed, you and Noah break out the buckets. You too, young fellow." He pointed at Sam. "Form a line and throw water onto that fire, fast!"

Fire! For a few seconds Amity stood transfixed, remembering the other blaze that had brought the end of her happy world three years before.

Suddenly she thought of her father! Surely he must have heard the shouting. She scanned the deck frantically but among the hurrying men there was no sign of Darius Lyte. Could he be still asleep?

Tim clung tightly to her hand, his eyes terrified. Clearly, he too remembered that other fire, though he'd been only three years old at the time. She pried his fingers loose. "Tim, you stay here. I must wake Father."

Then she was flying down the deck. The doors of the companionway leading to the passengers' cabins were closed. She yanked them open. Instantly a cloud of acrid yellow billowed out. She drew back, filled her lungs with clear air, and plunged down the ladder-like stairs.

The main cabin was a mass of white fog. Her eyes smarted from the fumes. She stumbled against a table, then felt her way to her father's compartment. There was the knob. She tore the door open and groped for the berth. Her fingers felt waistcoat buttons. She grasped the bony shoulders and shouted, "Father!"

It had been a mistake to cry out. The smoke knifed into her open mouth and throat. She felt for his face and slapped his thin cheeks. He coughed, choked, and sat up. "What's all this?" he muttered, rising groggily to his feet.

Amity had no breath to answer. She took his hand and pulled him into the main cabin. He stumbled over a chair and fell. She tugged at his arm until he got his feet under him again. Half supporting him, she fought her way across the room. The smoke seemed denser than ever. Her lungs pained with the effort of breathing.

Ah, there was the opening to the companionway. Could she manage to get her father up its steep steps? He was falling back, sinking to the floor. She must keep him moving. With all the strength she could muster she seized him under the arms and dragged him to the narrow stairway. A breeze flicked down a current of cool air. For a moment the smoke lifted and Darius Lyte raised his head. Amity got behind him and started to push him upward, clawing at the stairs. For all his thinness, his body had a surprising weight. One step, then another. She could see a pale streak of light above. One more step. Still another.

Just when she thought her lungs would burst with the strain she saw a glimmer of sun, and gave one last mighty shove. Darius Lyte slid forward in an ungainly sprawl onto the open deck. Amity pulled herself up after him and fell, gasping, on the bleached boards.

Weak as a newborn kitten she lay there while the breeze whipped the smoke away. Gratefully she drew in great gulps of clear fresh air.

Darius Lyte raised himself up and staggered to the rail, racked by fits of coughing. His eyes were red and streaming.

Amity could feel tears running down her own cheeks. Were they only because of the smoke? Suppose she had been too late? What if Father were still lying in his berth? She peered at his tall, gaunt figure, at the narrow face with its cap of smooth dark hair. Scrabbling to her feet, she tottered toward him. She had just reached his side when a muffled roar sounded from below, followed by a brisk crackle. The smoke in the companionway was lit by flames. They had escaped not a moment too soon!

Amity looked up into her father's face. Was gratitude too much to expect? If not that, at least he must share the relief that was flooding over her.

But there was no thankfulness in his gaze, only bitter, unmistakable regret. If there was anything more, it was rebuke. As clearly as if he were speaking, his eyes said, "Why couldn't you have let me die?"

Then he turned away, and she went to find Tim, hardly knowing where she stepped for the tears that blinded her.

2

Across the Mudflats

Half an hour later Amity perched precariously on the *Rover's* rail, one hand clenched on a stay as she mustered the courage to jump. From behind came the roar and crackle of flames. The fire fighters' desperate efforts had checked the fire's progress only long enough for the captain to coax the disabled vessel toward the Connecticut shore. Moments ago the bow had nosed into a water-covered mudbank a half mile out from land, not far from Guilford, the captain said.

Amity looked down. Standing in the shallow water below were the crew and Sam Baldwin, their arms upstretched. Almost overcome by vertigo, she took a firmer grip on the rigging. What a fearful drop! The water must be fifty feet away. She could never jump that distance!

Behind her the captain shifted impatiently between her father and Tim. "Jump, girl! Hurry!" he roared.

If she must, she must. She took a deep breath, and leaped. Her black slippers, dangling from her neck by their long ties, flew up across her sunburned cheek. Her muslin skirt billowed up. Only the strings kept her bonnet from sailing away.

Then her bare feet knifed through the water, and strong hands steadied her as she tried to get a footing in the ooze. The cook was on one side of her, his face dark with soot and worry. How slippery the mud was! Her feet sank through slime and met the sharp edges of shells. Involuntarily she put out a hand to the nearest shoulder. It belonged to Mr. Samuel Baldwin. Strong teeth flashed white in his smoke-streaked face, and his dark eyes showed admiration and concern.

"I trust you're not hurt, Miss Lyte?" he asked.

"N-No," she faltered, breathless from the leap and the shock of the cold water, and shaking with the fear that had gripped her. Still holding to Sam's shoulder, she turned and looked back up at the ship where the captain held Tim in his arms, ready to drop him over the side. They seemed very near. Had the vessel sunk lower in the water? Surely the distance could be no more than twenty feet. Tim looked down at her, his eyes enormous in his narrow face.

The captain gave a heave, and the boy hurtled downward. Two of the sailors caught him and set him on his feet next to Amity. She put her arm around him in comfort. If only he would not feel her own trembling.

Together they watched Darius Lyte clamber awkwardly over the rail, grip it in both hands, then drop. A moment later Captain Abbot landed on the mudbank beside him, his stocky body throwing up a geyser of salt water, thoroughly soaking what little of Amity's clothing had been dry.

"We'd best get moving!" the captain shouted. "It's a

good half mile to dry ground, and I don't relish being caught on these flats in the dark." He squinted at the low-lying sun.

Behind him the fire gained headway. Quick thunder sounded, and the forward hatch cover sailed into the air, borne upward on a fiery cloud.

"There goes the flour, blast it! Twelve dozen barrels of the best Philadelphia superfine," growled the captain, his face twisted in helpless anger.

"Lookit that blaze!" shouted the cook. "A danged good thing we got off when we did." He gave a hitch to his pants, and spat out of the corner of his mouth.

For a few minutes the group waited, the heat of the fire warm upon their skins. The wind had dropped, and the flames were reflected in the still water. Amity stared at the burning hull and shivered. The shooting flames seemed to mock her. Would disaster and horror follow this fire as they had the one just after her mother's death?

With Tim's hand tight in hers, she floundered through the water, her long skirt swirling about her ankles and clinging to her legs. With each step her feet sank through the mud. It was not only slimy; it was slippery. And the shells embedded in it cut like knives.

She looked landward across the broad stretch of water to a green marsh bordered by woodland. Birds soared above it, darting down now and then, their cries thin in the distance. The sun's rays shone almost horizontally, lighting the shipwrecked company. They were a scarecrow lot, singed and soot-blackened. Darius Lyte seemed a caricature of himself, with wet trousers clinging to his bony shanks, looking like a giant crane.

One of the seamen stumbled and fell. He scrambled to

his feet and slapped at his drenched clothes. Cursing, he shook his fist at the now smoldering sloop. Its timbers sizzled and hissed as they struck the water.

Still clinging to Amity's hand, Tim said anxiously, "Do you think we'll get to land before dark?" She followed his glance to the west. The sun was sliding behind the clouds. In a minute it vanished, leaving behind a cold gray chill. Though Tim forced his thin legs manfully, he made but slow headway. Gradually the captain and crew were drawing ahead.

"Make believe you're a giant, Tim, and try to take longer steps," she said. It was hard to keep her voice calm. The light was fading, and the shore seemed an interminable distance away.

"Perhaps your brother would like to ride horseback, Miss Lyte." Sam Baldwin spoke from behind them.

"Horseback?" echoed Tim. "I don't see a horse. Besides, I don't know how to ride one."

"This horse isn't very fast, but he's steady," said Sam, bending over in front of Tim. "Come on, climb up on my back and put your arms around my forehead."

Tim clambered up, shivering and dripping. Sam forged ahead with an even tread. Amity found it hard to keep up. Her toes curled in revulsion with every step into the ooze.

"How can you go so fast?" she asked, forgetting that she had been forbidden to speak to him. "I'm afraid I'll slip if I hurry."

"Try putting your weight on your forward foot. And take a grip with your toes."

She tried it, and found new confidence.

"What if you do slip?" Sam asked with a grin. "You'll only get a bit wetter. I learned that when I worked at mowing grass in the canal bed. There's a trick to keeping your feet and swinging a scythe in three feet of water."

"What's a canal?" asked Tim.

"If you don't know what a canal is," said Sam, "you've asked the right person. The Middlesex Canal was begun when I was just about your size, and for ten years I watched it being built until it was finished a year ago. A canal is a big ditch dug to connect two bodies of water so that boats can carry cargoes long distances, perhaps from way inland down to seaports."

"Is it hard to dig?" asked Tim. He kept his hands clasped on Sam's forehead. Now he bent down to look into Sam's face.

"Indeed it is," answered Sam. "Sometimes the men have to cut through rock, sometimes through mud like this. Where the canal has to go uphill or downhill there are locks like a giant staircase where the boats can float up and down. And in some places the canal crosses over a river in a big trough called an aqueduct."

A canal crossing over a river? What a preposterous idea! Amity almost burst out laughing. Did Sam expect her to believe that? She'd like to hear what more his lively imagination could contrive.

"Did you say you worked on the canal?" she asked.

"Since I was just a bit older than Tim," he replied, shifting the boy's weight on his shoulders. "At first I was only allowed to carry instruments for my uncle. Then I delivered messages to the crews. Later I mixed mortar for the stonework and did other jobs."

"It sounds as if you had done about everything," said Amity. Could she believe him? It was hard to imagine a boy the size of Tim working.

"There was a lot I couldn't do," said Sam regretfully. "School took up a good deal of time."

"I don't like school," said Tim vehemently, and he kicked his heels against Sam's chest for emphasis.

"Hey, there, that's no way to treat a horse." Sam gave his rider a playful shake. "I didn't like school either when I was your age. But Uncle made me go."

"What about your father and mother? Didn't they want you to?"

"They died when I was small," he said. "I've lived with my uncle ever since."

"He certainly made you work hard," observed Amity. She was not prepared for Sam's outburst of laughter. His shoulders shook so that Tim bobbed back and forth.

"I would have been miserable if he hadn't let me," he said. "Uncle knows more about canals than anyone in this country. I thought it an honor, and a great chance to learn."

"Your uncle must be a very important man," said Amity.

"I daresay he is," answered Sam. "He was the First Sheriff of Middlesex County, and now he's a Special Justice. He's been a Representative to the General Court, and head of about every town committee in Woburn. And Superintendent of the Middlesex Canal. It's easy to tell you're not from Massachusetts. Most everybody there has heard of Colonel Loammi Baldwin."

Darius Lyte had been walking some distance to the left, his long legs scissoring through the water. Now he halted and stared at Sam. "So Loammi Baldwin is your uncle!" His tone was icy. "Timothy, the water is shallow enough for you to walk easily now. Get down at once.

Amity, I fear you have forgotten my injunction not to speak with this young man."

Sam's face was a study in bewilderment. As he set Tim down his puzzled hurt was evident. Amity felt resentment rising within her. Why was Father behaving so rudely? Mr. Baldwin had been kindness itself, and Father had dismissed him with an abruptness he would not have shown to a servant. She would have liked to apologize to Sam, or at least to thank him. But her father was glowering at her.

She watched the young man move ahead with long strides. Dejectedly she slowed her pace to Tim's. The mud seemed stickier, and there were more shells. She winced as her foot struck a sharp edge. For a few minutes, while Sam was talking, she had almost forgotten her discomfort. Now it struck her with fresh misery.

Soon the water came just to her ankles. Marsh grass poked stiff blades between her toes, but she hardly felt it, her feet were so numb. The water ended at the edge of a broad marsh and Amity stopped gratefully to put on her slippers. In the distance, a tiny pinpoint of light shone.

"Looks like we're in luck, folks." Captain Abbot's voice rang out. "There's a house ahead, and that means food and fire. We'll not sleep empty or wet tonight."

3

The Marsh Cottage

Amity sat at one corner of the broad hearth, the heat drawing steam from her wet clothing. With a wooden spoon she cleaned her plate of scrambled egg and corn meal mush. Tim leaned heavily against her, his eyes half closed.

Scattered about the broad plank floor were the other members of the *Rover*'s company, intent upon their food. Mr. Baldwin had chosen a spot as far from her as possible, Amity noted. In the flickering light his face still showed hurt puzzlement.

A wizened scrap of a man with a stumpy pipe between his teeth regarded the group through faded blue eyes. His wife, her wrinkled face beaming, walked stiffly from the buttery, two mugs in her hands.

"Here's milk for the young'uns," she said, handing one to Amity, the other to Tim.

Young ones indeed! Amity accepted the milk stonily. Did this little old woman think she was still a child? She started to sip slowly, but the milk was so fresh and creamy she was hard put to it not to gulp. From under crepy lids the woman's small brown eyes looked at her with such satisfaction that Amity found herself saying, "Nothing has ever tasted so good as this meal. It's perfect."

And so had been their welcome when they straggled up to the thatched cottage, dripping salt water and plastered with mud. The old man had met them at the door, a candle held high, for twilight had thickened into darkness as they toiled through the high marsh grass. Unseen creatures had twanged and whined. Mosquitoes and midges had tormented them, their bites like needle pricks.

"Figgered there might be some folks comin' ashore from that boat that burned. Gammer and Gaffer Foote is allus glad to help out in time of trouble. And there ain't no trouble worse than a shipwreck," he had said.

His wife poked her head around his, her sharp features birdlike, and called in a cracked voice, "Don't keep 'em standing outside. Bring 'em in and let me get some victuals in 'em."

When Amity and Tim limped through the doorway, soaked and tottering, Gammer Foote chirped with delight. She untied Amity's sodden bonnet strings, unwound the long ties that held her slippers, and drew her to a low stool beside the fire. Too weary to protest, Amity accepted the warmth and attention. How long since anyone had fussed over her?

The men trooped in to stand about the fire. The captain was full of questions. Could the Footes give them a meal and lodging? He would pay them for their trouble. How near was the post road? When was the next stage due? His passengers would need transportation to Boston, and he must get back to New York to report the *Rover's* loss to the owners. The cargo and ship were insured. He trusted that his passengers had made similar provision for their effects. Sam nodded in assent. At the captain's questioning look, Darius Lyte said, "No."

"That's a pity," said the captain. "I hope you hadn't brought much with you."

Only everything we owned, thought Amity. Three trunks and a box of books. The future loomed empty and uncertain. She turned her mind away from it, too tired to think of anything. She could feel her head drooping, her eyelids closing. Then she awoke with a jerk. The men were filing toward the door, Gaffer Foote in the lead saying, "There's plenty of fresh salt hay in the barn. 'Twill make a fine soft bed fer ye."

Gammer Foot headed for the bedroom. "Come give me a hand with the trundle bed, dearie. We'll bring it out here so you and the boy won't be kept awake by my man's snoring."

The trundle bed was a light framework laced with rope and overlaid with a corn-husk mattress and feather bed.

"Now here's a shift for you and an old shirt for the boy." Gammer Foote peeled Tim's damp clothes from his body. "My land, he's a rack of bones. Needs feeding up, he does. Your mother's dead, I reckon."

"These three years past," said Amity. She didn't trust herself to say more.

"Lucky the boy's got you to look after him." Gammer Foote bundled the shirt about Tim and rolled him onto the bed. She turned to Amity. "Don't waste any time getting in there yourself." She brushed her lips across the top of Amity's head with a touch as light as a butterfly's wing. "I do miss having my own girl around." Then she was gone.

Amity was just falling asleep when a rumbling snore jerked her back to wakefulness. Did Gammer Foote think a mere door could confine such a racket? The thin planks acted more like a sounding board. To the heavy rumble was now added a high, squeaking rasp. Gaffer wasn't the only Foote who snored! Amity lay listening to the discordant duet until the day's stresses took their toll, and she slept.

She awoke to the tug of Gammer's hand on her shoulder. "Best get up now. The men'll soon be in looking for their breakfast." She held up a shapeless garment faded to a gray lavender. "You can put this on. I expect you'll want to rinse the salt out of your clothes and your menfolks' too."

After breakfast Captain Abbot was all business. He pulled a canvas sack from his pocket and counted out coins for Darius Lyte and Sam. "Your passage money," he said. "It'll take most of that to get you to Boston." He replaced the sack, adding, "Anyone want to walk to Guilford to make arrangements for the stage?"

"I'll go," Sam offered quickly.

I don't blame him, thought Amity. If I'd been treated as he was yesterday, I'd want to get away, too. She noticed that Sam had carefully avoided each member of the Lyte family.

"The rest of you do what you've a mind to," the captain said. "I've got some figgering to do."

"I'd like to dig a mess of clams," said the cook.

"There's a fork and basket in the shed," said Gammer Foote. "I've got salt pork and onions just cryin' to go into a chowder." She trotted out.

"You, boy," the cook said over his shoulder, "want to come along?"

Tim shook his head. "I'm going to help take the cow to pasture, and maybe ride on the wagon later." He went out with Gaffer Foote, the borrowed shirt drooping off his shoulders.

Amity and her father were the only ones left in the cottage. He brushed at his trousers and looked sourly at his wrinkled coat and stained shirt.

"I wonder if you could buy a new suit in the town where the stage comes in?" Amity said.

"I haven't the money," he answered tersely. "The refund on our passage is all I have."

"All you have!" she echoed. Surely he had had extra money when they set out.

"I put my funds into the trunk for safekeeping," he said with a grimace.

Amity felt as if the floor had dropped out from beneath her. It was bad enough to lose their belongings, but to be without money was far worse. She rejected the thought of buying new clothes. She must make the only garments they owned as presentable as possible.

At the well she drew water and poured it into iron pots to heat over the fire. Gammer Foote helped lift a wooden tub into the yard. "You can do your wash outdoors," she said cheerfully. "I'll give yer pa some of my man's duds to wear."

Under her direction Amity soaked and scrubbed and rinsed, rubbing at muddy spots until her knuckles were raw. With the help of strong yellow soap, she conquered the stains.

"Now spread yer things on that grass in the sun, and they'll bleach white as strawberry blossom." Gammer Foote paused, her face screwed into a smile. "If yer hair ain't the purtiest sight ever, all shining like gold!"

Back in the house Gammer Foote sat beside a spinning wheel, pulled a strand of flax from a bundle of tow, and fastened it to the spindle. One foot pushed the treadle, the wheel turned, and like magic, the strand was twisted into thread.

Amity watched, fascinated. "Is that hard to do?"

Gammer Foote peered at Amity from under sparse brows. "You mean to say a great girl like you can't spin?"

"I never learned," admitted Amity. "I guess my teachers didn't think it was important."

"Important? Hmph!" sniffed the little woman. "Why, during the Revolution, how do you think I kept my young'uns and my man warm and decent when there wasn't an ell of cloth to be bought, let alone cash to pay for it? If I hadn't known how to spin—land sakes! Come here, child." She beckoned Amity to sit beside her.

"You take a piece of tow between your fingers—like this."

Amity held the fibres between her thumb and forefinger.

"Now you give the wheel a turn, and keep the thread taut, and pull it out, that's the way. Now let it wind up on the spindle. There, you've spun a length of thread."

"It's really not very hard." Amity looked up in pleasure.

"You've got a real knack for spinning, I must say," the

woman said admiringly. "Watch out, now, that you don't let any slub creep in—a lump, there, like that." She pointed to a thick spot on the thread. "That'll make a rough place in your cloth."

Soon Gammer Foote rose. "No need for me to sit by you. You're a natural-born spinner. I'll start that chowder." She vanished into the pantry, came back with a cube of salt pork, diced it, and dropped it into a large pot over the fire. She peeled and chopped onions, and added them. A tantalizing aroma filled the room.

The cook appeared with a crock of clams. Gammer Foote inspected them. "You went and shucked 'em without my even askin', bless you. And you cut the necks off and took the blacks out!" She poured the crock's contents into the mixture, gave it a stir with a wooden spoon, added creamy milk, then swung the pot away from the flames.

"We'll let it set till suppertime to give the clams and pork a chance to get friendly-like."

After dinner there was the ironing. Gammer Foote brought out a flatiron, placed it near the fire to heat, and spread a worn blanket on the trestle table. Amity smoothed Tim's small shirt and breeches, then her father's shirt and long white stock. Finally she ironed her petticoats and muslin dress and hung them over a rack, snowy white and clover-scented. Her father's coat and trousers she brushed and sponged and pressed with a dampened cloth. They looked far from elegant, but they were passable.

Each time Darius Lyte started to speak, Amity listened intently. Far back in her mind an inward ear was waiting. He need not make an open expression of gratitude for her action of yesterday. Just a special nuance, a touch of his hand, a glance would satisfy her. But she listened in vain. C665106 CO. SCHOOLS

Late in the afternoon Amity went to look for Tim. Tired of following after Gaffer Foote, he had wandered off. She made her way toward the marsh where a gentle breeze rippled through the tall grass, swallows dipped and soared, and the tang of salt mingled with the fragrance of blossoming shrubs. She found Tim flat on his stomach, watching with fascination a score or more of fiddler crabs. The crayfish scuttled with asymmetrical gait, each managing one small and one oversized claw with ludicrous agility. Tim held out a piece of grass. Grotesque pincers snapped shut and a crab moved off bearing the grassy spear, while Tim crowed with pleasure. Rolling over on his back he squinted up at Amity and said, "I don't want to go away from here—not ever."

She lay down on the grass beside him. How warm the sun was. It seemed to soak through her skin into her very bones. She closed her eyes and gave a long sigh, wishing the day could go on forever, with its warmth and sunlight and drowsy drone of crickets.

When she awoke, Tim was standing over her. "Something's coming," he announced. "I can hear horses."

Reluctantly, she followed him toward the cottage. The clip-clop of hoofs, the jangle of harness, and the rattle of wheels sounded distinctly. As they stepped into the clearing, a pair of horses came into view, pulling a carriage with seats along either side. In the driver's seat, reins in his hands and a broad smile on his face, was Sam Baldwin.

"The stage for Boston is due at Guilford tomorrow,

and the innkeeper let me hire this rig for the six-mile drive to town."

Supper was a triumph. The cook smacked his lips, sighed gustily, and said, "Best chowder I ever et. Seems as though some good comes out of every mishap."

The captain glared at him.

The cook went on hastily, "Didn't I see a fiddle hangin' up in the shed? Mind if I scrape ye a tune?"

Soon the notes of "Turkey in the Straw" rang out. "Come on, folks, up on your toes. Let's see a little high steppin'," called out the elderly host.

Captain Abbot bent his solid torso before Gammer Foote. "May I have the honor, ma'am?" he asked.

She stole a quick look at her husband, then with a toss of her birdlike head, rose and picked up the folds of her skirt.

Amity watched Sam out of the corner of her eye. Would he ask her to dance? She saw him rise, and then another figure stood before her. The steward, in perfect imitation of the captain, blurted, "May I have the honor, ma'am?"

She couldn't hurt his feelings. In a few minutes she was whirling in the steps of a reel. Had she thought she was tired? The gay tune drove away all fatigue. Her feet skipped over the floor as if they had not toiled over miles of mudbank the day before.

Two sailors cavorted together, one simpering and posturing with outspread elbows and mincing like an affected belle. In a corner Sam was showing Tim the steps for a reel. In the other corner a sailor was doing the hornpipe, his arms akimbo, his soles slapping with a merry rhythm.

The fiddler stopped, and the group flung themselves down on benches and stools and wide pine boards. Tim was laughing. "Dancing is fun!" he exclaimed.

Darius Lyte, in a shadowy corner, said nothing.

The cook took up the fiddle again, and called out, "All hands on deck for the Virginia reel."

With one bound Sam was at Amity's side. "Will you do me the honor?" he asked.

Amity could feel her father's presence like a dark cloud. In her mind she could hear again his injunction not to speak with this young man. But dancing was not speaking. She need not say a word. With a smile she swept him her best curtsey, lifting the faded lavender folds of her borrowed gown.

Then they were standing opposite one another, clapping their hands and stamping their feet in time to the squeaky notes. The simpering sailor was beside her, twisting himself into a caricature of feminine grace, quirking his little fingers.

Amity couldn't remember so gay a time. Dancing parties at school were stiff affairs, where the girls did the minuet and Portland Fancy with brothers and cousins under the teachers' watchful eyes. What with rigid stays and tight slippers, she'd scarcely enjoy a step. Tonight, with bare feet and her hair loose, wearing the borrowed gown, she could bound about freely. Laughing with excitement, she ducked her head and skipped under the archway formed by the upraised arms of the two lines of dancers. As they reached the end of the line, Sam took both her hands in his and swung them up high, giving her a bright smile.

"I never thought a shipwreck would lead to such a

good time," he said, "and to such good company." He
stopped abruptly as if he had said more than he intended.
His face was bright red in the firelight. Amity could
feel his grasp on her fingers tighten. Was his heightened
color due to the dancing? Or might it be for another
reason?

Then the two sailors pranced beneath their arched
arms, and the moment ended.

4

The Stagecoach

Wedged between her father and Tim, Amity braced her feet as the coach jolted over the rough road. After three days' travel she felt that every bone in her body had jarred loose. Enviously she watched Tim rub his small backside and wished she could as freely soothe her own.

Directly opposite loomed the formidable bulk of Mrs. Hepzibah Worthington, arbiter of propriety from New York to Boston, from whose lips issued one important name after another. She interrupted the recital only to declaim upon the terrors of travel.

Some of the inns along the post road were a scandal, she declared, little better than pigpens. More than mosquitoes had raised those bites on her body the night before. If there was anything worse than a bedbug she didn't know of it. How lucky Sam was, up front with the driver and out of earshot, thought Amity.

Not only had Mrs. Worthington passed a miserable night, but she had made sure that everyone else suffered with her, raising her voice in loud complaint. Only the landlord, thumping on the floor of his room overhead, had been able to silence her. After crouching sleeplessly on the edge of the bed they shared, Amity had rolled up in a quilt on the floor and got some fitful rest.

"Did you ever taste such wretched meals?" Mrs. Worthington leaned forward and tapped Darius Lyte on the knee.

He jerked his leg away, muttered, "Rarely," and resumed his stony stare out the window. The bucking vehicle took a sharp lunge.

Mrs. Worthington kept on. "I've heard the name Lyte before," she said. "Wasn't a Lyte well known a few years back? I connect him with the Hamiltons somehow."

Darius Lyte made no sign that he had heard. Amity tried to keep her face expressionless. Her father hated any prying into his past. If there were any way of escaping this busybody, he would have taken it long ago.

"Lyte—that is your name, isn't it? Now where have I heard it before?" Mrs. Worthington paused. Suddenly she exclaimed, "I have it now. Darius Lyte. He was a limner, and painted likenesses of the most fashionable people. That's why I thought of the Hamiltons. He did portraits of them both." She leaned forward until her prominent nose almost touched Amity's. "Are you related to him by any chance?"

Amity felt her father's elbow dig into her side. She couldn't lie. "In a way," she murmured. The lady was too engrossed with her own recollections to heed the reply.

"There was a strange story about that Darius Lyte,"

she went on. "I've often heard of him, though we've never met. One day he was successful, and friendly with the best people. Then something happened, and he dropped out of sight. Nobody ever saw him again. Portraits he had begun he didn't finish. And soon people forgot all about him."

"Perhaps that's the way he wanted it," offered Amity through clenched teeth. How she would like to stuff Mrs. Worthington's fine linen handkerchief into her meddlesome mouth, and tie her scarf around her pendulous cheeks so that she couldn't so much as move her tongue behind her yellowed teeth! The woman had opened up the old scar, and Amity was fighting tears and her own gaping loss.

How clearly she remembered the days Mrs. Worthington spoke of! Her father had been the successful limner she described. In his studio on the top floor of their home he had painted portraits of fashionable ladies and distinguished gentlemen, while their waiting coachmen walked their horses up and down outside. Amity could remember her father content and happy. His hair had been jet-black then, not iron-gray. His step had been lively, and he had been full of love and concern for them all, especially for her mother, her lovely, gracious mother who made everyone feel cherished. Merely to be in the same room with her had made Amity joyous. And her brothers, all three—how they had adored their mother. Though Tim, the youngest, was little more than a baby then.

In summer weather the yellow fever had struck. Her parents had planned to move out of the city, but her father wished to finish a portrait. And her mother would not go without him. Another day or two would make little difference, she claimed.

The day or two had cut their family in half. Her mother and the two older boys had sickened with the dread fever. Then, in so short a time, all three were dead. Afterward, Darius, fearful lest Amity and Tim become infected by something the others had touched, flung most of their possessions—clothing, toys, books, linens, even furniture—onto one towering heap and set fire to it. In a frenzy of fear and guilt he had fed the flames, throwing upon them his paintings too, even the unfinished portraits.

Amity had watched from an upper window, Tim clinging to her and screaming in fear. The flames had left their mark upon her mind as surely as if their heat had seared her flesh.

From that day onward Darius Lyte had sat in his studio, his head in his hands, day after day after day. Neither Amity's pleas nor Timothy's tears could penetrate his grief. A succession of servants took advantage of his apathy, pilfering what valuables remained, stealing the house money, and neglecting the children.

On Amity, then thirteen, had fallen all the care of three-year-old Tim. She had tried to take her mother's place, and found some comfort in caring for the small boy, lavishing on Tim all her love for the two older boys. No one would ever know how deeply she missed them —and her mother. Night after night she awoke from a dream in which the family was reunited, and found her pillow wet with tears.

For two years Darius Lyte rarely stepped outside his

studio. Finally nothing remained but debts. A friend helped with the sale of the house and its contents, and urged Darius to resume his work of portraiture. He flatly refused. He'd never touch brush to canvas again, he asserted. Painting had robbed him of his wife and sons; he wanted no more of it.

Confronted by necessity, he was forced to take a position at Miss Reed's school teaching calligraphy. His formation of letters was so elegant that his work soon won approbation.

From the outset Amity had hated the school and her own uncertain status there, midway between pupil and servant. When the other girls filed out on afternoon promenades, Amity had to remain behind to tidy the classrooms or help the French mistress. How particular Mlle. Armand had been, admonishing Amity in precise syllables when she failed to correct an accent grave or acute. Amity grew to respect the immaculately groomed Huguenot for her uncompromising standards, and to be grateful for her interest.

"You have a quick mind and a good ear, Amity. Soon you may become a teacher yourself."

At first Amity had regretted not being able to promenade with the other girls. Later she was glad to escape their chatter. How they bragged of their fathers' exploits during the Revolution! "My father was with General Washington." "My father was aide to Lafayette." "My father was at Yorktown."

Then would come the inevitable question. "What was your father's regiment, Amity?" And her own reply in a low voice: "My father didn't fight in the war."

Their eyes would widen. "Oh, he must be a Friend."

"He's not a Quaker," she said.

There were covert glances. Then one more daring than the rest blurted, "He must be a Tory!"

"A Loyalist!" said another, her tone accusing and deadly. What could be worse, even twenty-three years after the war had ended, than to have been opposed to the glorious cause of freedom? Loyalist. Tory. Traitor. No other words conveyed such opprobrium. A man could be a cheat, a liar, a murderer even, and not be so deeply hated as one who had fought against the American colonies, or refused to fight in their behalf.

"He was not a Tory," she had said as quietly as she could, though the blood flamed in her face and she could feel her pulse pounding. "My father just doesn't believe in violence and killing."

"Not even for the cause of liberty?" Their lips made the word sacrosanct. Chins went up. Noses tilted high. The group moved away and began anew. My father this. My father that. Amity fled to her room, saying fiercely to herself, I don't care, I don't care. But in her heart she had been ashamed.

Other times they would talk of their families. "My great-great-grandfather was one of the first settlers of New York." "My mother was born in Virginia." "I'm descended from the Oglethorpes of Georgia." Innocent eyes would turn to Amity. "What part of the country is your family from?"

When she hesitated, one would gibe, "Don't you know who your grandparents were? Your father must have been a foundling."

"Certainly not," she would deny. But inwardly she wondered. Other girls had grandparents, aunts, uncles, and cousins of varying removes, a wide circle tied by bonds of blood and love. If only she had one relative with whom she could share her concern for her father and Tim. Just one who would listen with a whole heart and mind to her thoughts—one person who cared.

She never mentioned the conversations to her father. She saw him only in the classroom, where he favored her the least of his pupils for fear of showing partiality. He was harsh in his criticism of her handwriting, insisting that she do a paper over and over until she was ready to rip it to bits.

Her only bright spots were visits to Tim at the house where he boarded. But even those had turned to torment. How could one explain to a weeping child who begged to go home that there was no home to go to?

When Miss Reed announced her impending marriage and the closing of the school, Darius Lyte made ineffectual efforts to secure another post. Word came of a scandal at a Boston school conducted by Mrs. Snow, a friend of Miss Reed. Her calligraphy teacher had dared to elope with one of his pupils. Miss Reed wrote immediately to her friend, recommending Darius Lyte as an older man less likely to attract the affections of young girls. On this uncertain premise he had set out for Boston.

As the coach jolted along, Amity found herself willing the horses to go faster. She could hardly wait to get to Boston. At the marsh cottage the shipwreck had seemed an adventure, but now their plight was taking on the aspect of a nightmare. Gradually the extent of their loss became real to her.

Her trunk hadn't held much; her possessions were modest. But they were her own, and the longer she did without her brush and comb, her night rail, shoes, and shawls, the more she missed them. The loss of her father's trunk was more serious. Men's clothes were of importance in their work, especially in teaching, where pupils regarded critically a loose button or frayed cuff. Worse was the loss of his money.

The coach was traveling along a sandy road. Amity brushed dust from her frock. Though she had made every effort to keep it clean, days of summer heat and rain had reduced the white dress to a limp, grimy gray.

Mrs. Worthington had sunk her chin in the folds of her neck and was breathing heavily. Amity thought of lucky Sam sitting beside the driver. How she wished she could be there, out in the open air with a cool breeze blowing upon her face.

Tim shifted his position. "Are we almost there, Amity?" he whispered.

As if in answer, the driver bawled, "You can see Boston from the top of the next hill. Will the gentlemen please to get out and walk?"

He slowed the horses. Tim was on his feet and out the door in a trice. Darius Lyte followed, and after him went Amity, avoiding Mrs. Worthington's disapproving glare. Sam climbed down from the box and strode ahead, whistling cheerily. Tim ran to catch up with him, heedless of his father's frown.

I wish I could go with them, thought Amity. Instead she walked beside her father, picking each step with care. Her slippers were not meant for tramping on country roads. She must tread lightly lest their thin soles wear through.

The horses toiled up the slope, dragging the unwieldy

vehicle in which Mrs. Worthington, looking like a fat Buddha, was jostled about. Ah, here was the top of the hill. And there were Tim and Sam, sprawled on the ground, their heads propped on a log, gazing at the scene before them.

The hilltop had been cleared of trees, and the travelers could look down a long hillside to a winding river. Beyond was a glimpse of ocean and three hills bristling with chimneys and wreathed in smoke.

"Yonder's Boston," said the driver, pointing his whip. "In two hours we ought to be there. Step lively now. Everybody aboard."

5

An Accident

The tired horses put on a burst of speed and the stage soon drew up with a toot of its horn at Daggett's Inn in Dock Square. Mrs. Worthington descended ponderously, demanding that the porter get her luggage out of the boot and into the tavern at once. Sam Baldwin jumped lithely to the cobblestones. As Amity placed her foot on the high step of the coach, he offered a hand to assist her.

"Is there anything I can do for you, Miss Lyte?" he asked. "One of my cousins lives in Boston, and he'd be glad to help."

He must suspect they were in trouble. Had Tim said anything? But Tim really knew nothing of their plight.

"Oh, no," she said quickly. "My father is going to teach at Mrs. Snow's school. As soon as we get there we'll be all right." She felt stiff and dizzy from the long ride, and confused by the crowds of people jamming the square. Some were jostling for places on the stage just ahead, which the driver was announcing was due to leave for Cambridge in three minutes.

"Well, I just thought—losing your luggage and all—" Sam's voice trailed off.

"Amity," called Darius from the other side of the coach.

"I must go now," she said. "Thank you for being so kind—to Tim. Good-by, Mr. Baldwin."

He looked at her anxiously as if loath to see her go.

"Amity." Her father sounded impatient.

She brushed past Sam, giving him a quick smile, and went to her father. Out of the corner of her eye she could see Sam striding away with his quick, sure gait.

"Shall we go into the tavern?" she asked. "It might be well to spend the night here and see Mrs. Snow after we have rested."

Darius Lyte shook his head wearily. "Not enough money."

Amity smoothed back her hair, adjusted her bonnet, and shook out the folds of her skirt. She made Tim put out his tongue, pressed her handkerchief against it, and wiped his face. He wrinkled his nose in distaste.

"That's a cat wash, Amity," he complained.

"It's better than nothing," she said crossly. She passed the handkerchief to her father. "There's a smudge on your cheek," she said.

His hand, when he took the linen square, was trembling. She could see his jaw muscles bunch as he wiped at his cheek. "We'll go directly to Mrs. Snow's," he said. "I'll discuss terms with her, and perhaps ask for an advance. In the circumstances, I don't see how she can refuse." He looked ruefully at his son and daughter. "Green Street lies along this way," he said, walking on ahead.

Amity and Tim followed through the crowded streets where brick and frame houses stood in tight rows. A two-wheeled cart rumbled past, laden with hogsheads. A farm wagon piled high with crates of cackling chickens jolted after it. Hawkers crying their wares jostled gentlemen in tall hats and long-tailed coats.

How does Father know the way? Amity wondered. He seemed very sure of where he was going. With every step she grew more certain that Darius Lyte knew Boston and knew it well. Was this city part of her father's mysterious past?

Tim skipped along beside Amity, peering into shop windows, staring at peddlers, asking one question after another.

They came to a broad street lined with stately houses. "This is Green Street," announced Darius Lyte. He pointed to a three-story wooden building, its front walk shaded by maples. "That is number twenty-two. It must be Mrs. Snow's Boarding School for Young Ladies."

Together the three approached the front door. White curtains fluttered in open windows. The tinkling of a spinet and a snatch of song ceased abruptly at Darius's knock. A maid in a pink and green striped uniform half opened the door, peering at them suspiciously.

"Will you please inform Mrs. Snow that Darius Lyte has arrived?"

Hesitantly the girl let them into a small vestibule. Then she went through an inner door and shut it behind her. She's judging us by our appearance, thought Amity. Couldn't she tell by Father's voice that he is a gentleman?

In a few minutes the maid led them into a small room

with a polished mahogany table in the center, on which stood a bowl of full-blown roses. Amity drew Tim beside her onto a sofa upholstered in wine velvet and looked up into a gilt-framed bull's-eye mirror over the mantel. Could those tired faces be hers and Tim's? She sat up, squared her shoulders, crossed her ankles, and folded her hands. She tried to assume a confident smile, though heaven knew she felt far from that.

Mrs. Snow came in. Short and plump, with a cloud of white hair, she had cheeks as pink as the roses on the table. Her brown eyes were filled with dismay, and she gasped as she looked at the three of them.

"Obviously you did not receive my letter. Oh, Mr. Lyte, I am sorry indeed." One dainty hand flew to her bosom. Her fingernails were as polished as seashells.

"Your letter, Mrs. Snow?" Darius Lyte looked down from his gaunt height.

"As soon as I heard from Miss Reed I wrote to her that I had already engaged a teacher of calligraphy, a young lady. It seemed advisable after my unfortunate experience to choose a woman. The letter must have miscarried. And now you have come all this way—and with your family, too. Oh, dear! Oh, dear!" She clasped her hands together, then went on, "Now, let me think. There are other schools in Boston. I could inquire if there is a post vacant. That's what I shall do, this very evening. And you must give me your address so that I can get in touch with you." When she smiled, her cheeks plumped out.

But we have no address, thought Amity. She looked helplessly at her father.

He stood dignified and composed. "Thank you, Mrs.

Snow. That will be very kind. I shall let you know where we are lodging. Good day." He started for the door.

Mrs. Snow fluttered after him. "I am so sorry, Mr. Lyte. I would not have had this happen for the world."

"It's quite understandable," he said smoothly. Amity gave Tim's hand a warning squeeze. If only he would not blurt out his disappointment. Somehow they got out the door and down the path. Darius Lyte paused, then turned down Green Street the way they had come. Amity followed him silently, Tim at her side.

They had walked two blocks when the accident happened. Darius Lyte was leading the way across an intersection. A frenzied horse bolted from a side street, a dilapidated hackney coach careening behind. Nostrils flaring, froth bubbling from its lips, the animal shot forward like an onrushing fury.

"Look out!" bawled the driver, sawing at the reins.

"Father!" screamed Amity, drawing Tim back on the sidewalk. But Darius Lyte, walking with bent head, seemed to hear nothing. While Amity watched, the horse rushed past, and the coach lurched, struck against her father, and flung him to the ground.

Instantly a crowd gathered. Curious, indignant citizens closed in around Darius Lyte.

"Those hack drivers—devils on wheels, they are!"

"A person hardly dare walk abroad these days for the danger!"

"A pity the law can't slow those fellows down. He must have been going at ten miles an hour!"

Amity bent over her father. There was a gash in his head, and his right arm was twisted beneath him at an unnatural angle. His face was ashen and his eyes closed. She tried to stanch the blood with her handkerchief.

"Father?" she said. "Father?" Her voice rose in fright. Surely he was not dead?

There was a shout at the perimeter of the crowd, and an angry voice cried, "Here comes the murderer now!"

Amity turned and saw a burly giant pushing his way through the throng, as if the people were so many cornstalks.

"Who's a murderer?" he demanded, and struck the man who had termed him that with a heavy blow on the shoulder. The man sat down heavily, his mouth open. "Can I help it if my mare bolts when a gull drops a clam on its back, shell and all?" continued the hack driver. "That gull was flying as high as the eagle on the monument when he let go his quahaug on poor old Jezebel. It must have carried a wallop like a musket!"

A burst of laughter rose. Darius Lyte's lashes fluttered as the huge man bent over him.

"Who's a murderer?" he repeated, throwing up his shaggy head triumphantly. "He's as alive as you and me." His lips parted to show broken teeth.

Amity's relief was as brief as it was instant. Darius Lyte gave a groan, and mumbled, "My arm." Then he sank back into unconsciousness.

"My father's badly hurt," said Amity. "I think his arm is broken." She didn't mention his head. Any fool could see the blood streaming past his ear, staining his neck-cloth and collar.

"We'd best get him to his lodgings," said the driver. "I'll take him there, even though it warn't my fault that danged Jezebel bolted. Nobody can say Bill Trask don't know his duty." He stooped down and picked up the unconscious man as easily as if he were a rag doll. Amity winced as the injured arm dangled. She opened the door of the hackney coach. It was far from elegant. Its dark-green paint was peeling, and what had once been gilded arabesques were painted over with canary yellow and enlivened by pink roses.

With surprising gentleness Bill Trask placed the limp figure on the seat. "Now where be ye bound?" he asked. "I'll take ye there, and if your father ain't come round by then, I'll fetch a surgeon."

Just where were they bound? Father had not told her what he planned to do or where he had been heading. What was the name of the inn where the stage had left them?

"Take us to Daggett's Inn," she said. Perhaps the proprietor would give them a room until her father could find a position. During the short drive she tried in vain to revive him. Her handkerchief was soaked with blood. Her heart was pounding and her palms clammy as she mopped at the wound with the ends of his stock. Darius Lyte lay inert, responding not one whit to her ministrations.

A dozen men were lounging around the shadowy room just inside the doorway of Daggett's Inn. Leathern mugs in hand, they looked up as Amity entered. Her head swam with the smell of ale and strong tobacco smoke. The proprietor hooked his thumbs under the edge of the vest that stretched taut about his barrel-like girth.

"What can I do for ye, Miss?" He swayed back on his heels and surveyed her with near insolence.

"I'd like rooms for my father and myself," she said stiffly.

"Well now, we've got the rooms. The question is, have you got the cash to pay for 'em?" He rocked forward on his toes with the question.

"I was going to ask about that," began Amity nervously. "My father is hurt, and there may be some delay in payment."

The eyes took on a cold gleam. "That's too bad, Miss, but I don't take travelers without hard money."

"But I told you he's injured. And we have nowhere to go." She fought to keep the panic from her voice.

"No money, no rooms." The man leaned back on his heels and looked over her head. "You ready for another noggin, Josh?" He headed for the bar at the room's far end.

Amity looked after him uncertainly, then around the room at the other men. Perhaps the stage driver was here; he might help her. She searched the faces. All were strange. All were avoiding her. She might as well have been invisible.

Bill Trask nodded his head as she came out. "Wouldn't give you credit, eh?" he said. "Ah, don't look so surprised. I could tell ye was down and out the minute I seed ye. Those innholders are a hard-hearted set of buzzards, blast their lights. Well, where be ye goin' now? Any friends in town?"

Amity was close to tears. Tim was cowering in a corner of the carriage, bewildered beyond words. Her father lay like a bundle of old clothes. What was she to do?

"Just because we've been shipwrecked and lost our trunks and money doesn't mean we're paupers."

"Ye've got some money ye can lay yer hands on?"

"I don't know," she faltered. "You see, my father—"

"He never told you. Uh-huh." Bill Trask shook the reins over the horse's back, and the coach began to roll.

"Where are you taking us?" demanded Amity. She had heard of workhouses and homes for paupers, squalid, sordid establishments, most of them. She shrank from the prospect.

"Fer now I'm takin' ye home with me. I don't know what else to do wi' ye. I can't just dump the old man out on the street. Though I fear what the missus'll say," Bill Trask said glumly.

The missus said plenty when they drove up to the ramshackle wooden house on Link Alley. Bill drove the coach into a shed adjoining the house, saying, "You stay here while I go see how the land lays."

Minutes later Amity listened in horrified fascination, longing to slip out of the carriage and run away. But she could not leave her father. And where could she run to?

A sharp, nasal voice stabbed through the air like a stiletto. "Not again! Bill Trask, are ye completely daft? You pickin' up more strays, and us with scarce enough to keep our young'uns fed. Where are we to put them? I'd like to know."

"Ah, Nance, have a heart. The old coot's not a sot. He's a gentleman, plain as the nose on yer face."

"You leave my nose out of this, Bill Trask. It's your stickin' yer nose into other people's business that's got us into trouble."

"Come on, Nance. Ye know ye've got a big, soft heart.

Else why did ye marry me?" There was a scuffle and a loud smack.

Then the woman's voice, muffled, said in a lower tone, "Well, just this one time more. But this is the last. From now on they go to the almshouse."

They came around the corner into the shed. She was a stout young woman with a tumbled mass of heavy blond hair that straggled over her face. At the sight of Tim and Amity, she drew back. "You didn't tell me there was a boy—and a grown girl!" she accused.

He shrugged his shoulders. "You know I never see any other gals but you," he said with a wide grin.

She hit out at him with a playful fist, then looked at Darius Lyte. At that moment he roused, half opened his eyes, and said, "Good day, madame."

Nance leaned an elbow on the carriage door. "Ye're right, Bill, he is a gentleman. Maybe enough of one to pay us for our trouble when he's to rights again. You can bring him into the back bedroom."

6

Decayed Gentlewomen

Any port in a storm, thought Amity, picking her way across a cluttered room between a broken hobbyhorse, a basket of shriveled potatoes, and a cracked leather boot. She tried not to wrinkle her nose at the smell of stale cooking fat and boiled cabbage, or to scowl at the two red-faced children squealing over a white mouse.

Nance Trask led the way to a small, gloomy room at the rear, its one window opening upon a dirty brick wall. The bed was covered with a rumpled quilt and children's garments. The woman swept them up, disclosing a lumpy mattress, and threw down a blanket and rough sheet.

"That's for him," she said. "You and the boy can make pallets on the floor. We'll bed the twins in our room."

"Thank you," said Amity. "It's very good of you to take us in." How hard to be gracious when gratitude was born of duty, and resentment threatened to engulf both. She bent to spread out the bedding. The linen sheet and the blanket, though coarse, were clean. She'd no sooner straightened up than Bill Trask carried in her father.

"Now I'll go fetch Doc Barrus," he said heartily. "Let's hope he's not got a skinful of rum."

The doctor was a spider-like creature with a round torso and bald head. While Amity held a basin of water, he cleansed the wound and bound it. Then he looked at her father's arm and said, "Aha!" Grasping Darius Lyte's right wrist, the doctor put one foot on the injured man's armpit and pulled on the broken arm with all his might. There was a sharp crack. Darius gave an agonized groan and relapsed into unconsciousness. Amity could feel her head swimming. Surely she was not going to faint. Gradually the room righted itself, and she could watch Dr. Barrus as he felt around the arm with knowing fingers.

"There, that's back in place again. I've seen worse breaks." He worked quickly with splints and linen strips. "It will be six weeks before I can remove the bandages, and a month more before he regains the proper use of the arm," he said. "Meanwhile keep him quiet."

Six weeks! And a month beyond that! The doctor might as well have said six years. How were they going to live for all that time?

The doctor was closing his valise. "I'm sorry we can't pay you now," said Amity. "We will, just as soon as we get some money."

Lying sleepless on her pallet that night, listening to her father's stifled moans, Amity tried to marshal her thoughts. Her father could not teach or do any kind of work in his present condition. How were they to live? Clearly she must find some way to earn money. She might serve as assistant in a girls' school as she had in New York.

At intervals through the night her thoughts turned to young Mr. Baldwin. How kind he had been to offer help. If his uncle—What was that queer name? Oh, yes, Loammi—was so important a man he might arrange a loan for her father until he could earn some money.

When she broached the subject in the morning, Darius Lyte turned upon her with cold anger. "Loammi Baldwin? He once doubted my word on a matter of the utmost gravity. He is the last person I would ask help from. I do not wish to have anything to do with him. And you have disobeyed me by talking with that young man."

There was no point in saying one couldn't obey such a command when escaping from a burning ship. Besides, Father had given her no valid reason for avoiding Mr. Baldwin. If he were a dangerous criminal or a teacher who eloped with pupils, she might have been willing to obey. But the flat order with no explanation had seemed senseless. All she was sure of was that her father had once known Loammi Baldwin and that they had disagreed about something. She knew better than to probe.

Soon Darius Lyte found the sleep he so badly needed. Amity must go about finding employment. As she walked through the main room, she heard Nance in the kitchen.

"Keep him quiet." She was mimicking Dr. Barrus. "And who's to pay for his food and his family's? That girl? When I was her age I'd been spinning in the loft for a year." She gave a derisive snort.

"Now, Nance." Bill's tone was placating. "Supposin' it was me lyin' there old and hurt? You wouldn't want some beauteous young woman to turn me out of her house, would ye?"

"Aw, Bill, gwan!"

Amity slid out the door. Tim, cradling the white mouse in his hands, was huddled beside the fence with Noah and Annie Trask. They had made a tent of a newspaper and were fighting over who could sit under it. Amity twisted her head to look at the date. It was yesterday's issue.

"I'll tell you a story if you'll let me read your paper," she offered.

The trio stopped squabbling. "Right now?" they asked.

"Just as soon as I look at the paper." She scanned the columns while the children leaned on her shoulders. Her eyes flicked over the advertisements. Ah, here was one.

WANTED in a small family, a young woman accustomed to cooking. Good recommendations will be required. Apply to the printers.

Her cooking had been limited to toast and tea. She could never fill that job. Here was something else.

WANTED: A steady young woman to take care of children. Inquire at office.

That would bear looking into. What else was there?

Mr. Barker begs leave to inform the public that he has opened a school in Spring Lane for the purpose of teaching Reading, Writing, Mathematics, Bookkeeping and Navigation. Hours for young gentlemen are from 8 a.m. until 11 a.m. and from 2 p.m. until 5 p.m. School hours for young ladies are from 11 a.m. until 1 p.m. and from 5 p.m. until 7 p.m.

Possibly Mr. Barker might be in need of an assistant. She would go to him immediately. She folded the paper and started to rise when three small voices cried, "Now the story!"

For fifteen minutes she recounted a lively tale of a brother and sister shipwrecked and cast ashore near a marsh where dwelt a little old man and woman who took them in and fed them and made them happy. When she stopped, Tim's eyes were shining. As Amity slipped away she could hear him telling of the wonders of the marsh, from fiddler crabs to Virginia reels.

That evening, when Amity took her father's emptied soup bowl into the kitchen, Nance met her with a smoldering look.

"Them that eats, works," she said in exasperation, pointing to stacks of dirty dishes.

Amity blinked. She had been so engulfed in her own woes she had not even offered to help. "If you'll show me where to wash them, I'll be glad to."

Nance pointed to a wooden tub leaning against a bench. "I take it you didn't find nothin' today," she said.

"No," said Amity. She didn't add that the woman had nine children and wanted her to live in. Or that the schoolmaster's tone had changed from cordiality to incivility when he learned that she was not a new pupil but was seeking a post.

"Where was it you used to work, Nance?" she asked, then blushed scarlet at this admission of eavesdropping.

"At the Boston Sail Cloth Manufactory on Frog Lane," said Nance proudly. "A great building it was, nigh onto two hundred feet. Fifty looms it had, and one hundred women spinning and as many girls turning wheels. It was a great sight. And noisy enough to split your eardrums, with the looms thumping and the wheels whirring."

"Do you think I could get work there?" asked Amity.

"It's been shut down these six years, more's the pity," said Nance.

When Amity went to fill the kettle she found the water barrel empty. That meant a trip to the well. The bucket left a trail of drops across the floor, making black puddles in the gritty dust. By then the fire had died down, so Amity built it up. While she waited for the water to heat, she tidied the room. Toys, shoes, and stockings littered the floor. Under the table was a pan encrusted with food. The table cloth was covered with spots.

Amity sank down on one of the chairs, heedless of the heap of soiled clothing upon it. She put her head in her hands and let discouragement sweep over her. Her feet and legs ached from walking on the uneven cobblestones. Her stomach was upset from the supper of fish and cabbage. Worst of all was her failure to find work. Whatever was she to do? The hissing of the kettle roused her. For the time being there was only one thing ahead. Those greasy dishes. Then she must get some rest. Far back in her mind a voice was saying, "Things will look brighter in the morning." That was good, she thought. They couldn't look any bleaker.

For ten dreary days Amity looked for work. During that time Darius Lyte lay listlessly in bed, accepting whatever food she brought him, saying little except when she told him of her search for employment. He protested that no daughter of his should so demean herself.

As the days went by Nance loaded more and more of the household work on Amity's shoulders. Not only was she expected to wash dishes, but linen as well. Ironing followed, and floor scrubbing. Amity could hardly find time to go to the newspaper office to ask if there were any advertisements for help. Many times she was too late, or so unfitted for the work that she was embarrassed to return. Only stubborn pride and desperate need drove her back day after day. She dreaded facing the pimply-faced youth who read off the notices to her—for a cook, a lady's maid, a milliner, a wigmaker.

"Isn't there something that requires less training?" she asked one day.

"The Blue Boar needs a scullery maid," he said with a smirk, and gave her directions.

A scullery maid. Had she come to that? She looked down at her hands, reddened and raw from strong soap, and at her cracked and worn slippers. Was she any better than a scullery maid at the Trasks' house?

The kitchen of the Blue Boar was like a steamy oven. Great joints of meat turned and sizzled at the enormous hearth. Bubbling kettles sent forth savory aromas. Cooks stirred, chopped, and kneaded, shouting to the kitchen boys to fetch more flour and make the ovens ready. Waiters hurried in and out, laden with trays. And in a dark pocket at one end of the bustling cavern was an array of tubs and drying racks nearly buried under a mountain of soiled plates and utensils.

The head cook looked at her dubiously, but said she could try out for the day. Then came nightmare hours of lugging pails, of plunging her arms into dishwater. She cut her finger on a knife; she slopped water as she staggered across the room with a heavy bucket.

What she hadn't been prepared for were the waiters

and busboys. A new girl was fair game for them all. They shouted at her for clean forks, for more dishes. One pinched her cheek and asked where she lived. Another gave her a hearty slap. What did he think she was? Her foot shot out and caught him on the shin. The tray he'd been carrying on his other hand fell to the floor with a crash of crockery.

"You needn't be so touchy," he said angrily. "It will take a day's tips to pay for these." He glared at her, and she returned the look, her eyes hot.

That night when she was leaving, the cook paid her twenty-five cents. "You needn't come back tomorrow," he said. "We need an older woman who won't cause such a stir."

Amity almost wept. "But I need the money badly."

"I can't have you working here," he said with finality.

Nance accepted the money grudgingly. "Mighty little for ten days' room and board," she said.

Two days later Amity again visited the newspaper office.

"I hear you caused quite a ruckus at the Blue Boar," said the pimply youth.

"Is there anything else?" asked Amity in an icy voice. If only he wouldn't leer at her that way.

"Nothing that would interest you," he said, "except possibly this one. But I don't know as you'd qualify." He laughed and pointed to a section of print with a dirty finger, the nail torn and ragged.

WANTED: Ten lady spinners and girl assistants. Only decayed gentlewomen need apply. The Zion Duck and Sail Cloth Company, Sun Court.

Decayed gentlewomen! Amity gave a rueful laugh. The words brought to mind a withered, brittle dame in rusty silks tottering with a gold-headed cane. Then she sobered. If decayed meant declined in fortune, she certainly qualified. As for being a gentlewoman, there was little in her present appearance to prove it. She'd have to rely on speech and manners.

Finding Sun Court was not difficult. From two blocks away Amity marked it by the queue of women on the pavement, and she almost turned back. Would she have any chance?

She was standing uncertainly at the end of the line when something plucked at her skirt. She looked down and saw a girl crouched in an alleyway, her small face upturned. She might have been twelve or fourteen years old. *"Mademoiselle?"*

"Oui." Amity's response was automatic.

"Ah, mademoiselle, vous parlez français!" The words came in a breathless rush.

"Seulement un peu," qualified Amity.

The girl beckoned her into the alley. *"Un moment,"* she said. Amity stepped into the shadows.

"Je suis émigrante," said the girl. She was small; her head with its crown of dark curls came just to Amity's shoulder. "It is *necessaire* that I find work *immédiatement.*"

"Moi aussi," said Amity.

"When I try to get work here they turn me away. They take only two people *ensemble,* I think. And they must be of *qualité.* I wait. I look to find someone of *qualité.* And now I find you. May I go with you, and then we may both be employed?"

An *émigrante.* There were plenty of them in the sea-

ports, refugees from the French Revolution or the Napo-
leonic regime. She looked closely at the girl. Was she telling the truth? Her dark hair was cut short in the French
fashion. Her dress of red silk was made in the Parisian
mode. It could not hide the thinness of her young body.
And the desperation in her dark eyes was real.

Two weeks ago Amity would have turned away from
the girl. Now she felt an instant rush of sympathy. She
would like to help her. And the girl might be right, that
only together could they be hired.

Footsteps sounded on the sidewalk. Amity took the
slender fingers. "Come on," she said, and darted back to
her place in the line just as a frowzy female in an orange
gown waddled up. They inched ahead. One after another,
disgruntled women stalked away. One, her red nose atilt,
said with a shrug, "Who's he to say I'm not a gentlewoman?" She flounced away, her purple petticoat switching in the dust.

Finally Amity's turn came. With the French girl beside
her she entered the building and turned into a small
office. Overhead sounded a cacophony of thwacks and
whirs. A fusty old man sagged in an armchair behind a
desk.

"Dear me," he sighed, "if only Obadiah Newcomb
wouldn't try to mix religion and business. Doling out jobs
like charity to ladies who have seen better days is not
my idea of a way to hire workers or make money. Who's
next?"

He looked at Amity over steel-rimmed spectacles.
"You're young for a decayed gentlewoman," he said,
waggling a finger.

"Not too young to have suffered a decline in fortune,"

said Amity. "My father is a limner, a gentleman, but he has an injured arm and cannot practice his profession. He and my brother and I were shipwrecked on our way from New York and lost everything, including our funds. My brother is too young to work. I am the sole support of my family, and if I do not obtain work soon, we will starve." That was true. Nance would not keep them indefinitely.

"That's a very sad story," said the man, "but I've heard so many lately I find it hard to believe. Have you any proof?"

"What proof could I have?" She could feel her face flushing. "You can come and see my father. Or you can write to Captain Abbot and ask him if we were passengers on the *Rover*."

"On the *Rover*, were you? A friend of mine came by stage with the survivors. You wouldn't recall her name?" His eyes were testing her.

"Do you mean Mrs. Worthington?" Unconsciously Amity mimicked the woman's tone of voice.

The man behind the desk laughed. "You know her, I can tell. Your story must be valid. Now, what about this girl? Is she your sister?"

For a moment Amity was tempted. What harm in claiming a false relationship? But if she lied now the man might doubt everything she had said. Better to be straightforward. "No, but she needs work as badly as I."

"What's your name? Amity Lyte? And the girl's?"

Heavens, she had not thought to ask her name. Amity looked at the puzzled face as the girl struggled to make sense out of the conversation. She knew something was expected of her.

"I am *émigrante*," she said haltingly.

"Amy Grey, eh? That's a good Boston name. Had a partner named Grey once, a fine man." He lifted a pen and scratched the two names on a paper.

"Report for work tomorrow at eight. I presume you can spin?"

"Yes," said Amity. She had spun some flax at Gammer Foote's. And the little woman had said that Amity had good fingers for it.

"You're sure now?" The man shot her a keen look.

"It's just that I haven't had much practice," she said.

"You'll get plenty of that," he said, bobbing his head up and down. "Amy Grey will turn the wheel for you. That will leave you two hands to spin with."

She was hired! She was going to work and would be paid for it! Amity couldn't remember leaving the office. Half a block away her head came down out of the clouds and she realized that the French girl was still with her.

"What is your name?" she asked, then repeated, "*Comment vous appellez-vous?*"

"*Je m'appelle Nicole Leseigner.*"

Où demeurez-vous?"

In answer the girl shrugged her shoulders and lifted her hands, palms up.

"Have you a family?"

Again the girl shrugged. "*Non.*"

"Where are you going now?" asked Amity.

"*Avec vous,*" said Nicole, putting her hand in Amity's.

"But I can't take you with me." Amity could see Nance's face, hear her outraged storm. She tried to pry the fingers loose, and the girl burst into tears, sank to the street, and clasped Amity about the knees.

"*Ayez pitié de moi. Mes parents,* they are dead. I hid on a ship to come to my Uncle René. But he had gone to Martinique. If I can but remain with you until he returns, all will be well."

No lies could be so convincing. Amity drew the girl to her feet. "Well, all right, just for a little while." With more trepidation than triumph she led the way to Link Alley.

7

The Spinning Loft

When Nance paused for breath in the midst of her expected tirade, Nicole darted forward and looked at the woman with unfeigned admiration.

"Ah, madame, vos cheveux sont magnifiques! Me permettez-vous de les arranger?"

Nance's anger turned to curiosity. "What'd she say?"

"You have magnificent hair and she would like to arrange it."

"But I'm just gettin' supper ready. I can't stop now." Plainly, though, Nance was mollified. She put one hand to the untidy blond mass.

"I'll do the cooking," offered Amity. "What had you planned?"

Nance sighed. "Oh, I don't know. I'm so tired of thinkin' what to eat. There's a fish Bill brought home. You could fry that."

It seemed as if they had been living on fried fish for a week. The kitchen reeked of it. Amity remembered Gammer Foote's chowder. She found salt pork in a barrel

71

and onions in the shed. And there was a full pitcher of milk. Soon she had a succulent potful simmering.

In the next room Nicole was chattering, brushing and combing and piling Nance's hair into thick coils. The three children sat on the floor.

"*Quels jolis enfants,*" cried Nicole. "They are handsome like their mamma, *non?*"

"They really take after Bill. But he's not ugly."

The tall bulk of the master of the house suddenly filled the doorway. "And who's calling me ugly, I'd like to know?" He regarded his wife. "Pretty fancy gettin' yerself a hairdresser, ain't ye?"

"Now, Bill." Nance poured out an explanation. She ended on a triumphant note. "The two of 'em are goin' to work tomorrow."

Nicole finished and stood back to survey her work. "You like, Madame?" she asked. Little Annie brought a cracked looking glass to her mother.

"I didn't know I'd caught me such a good-lookin' gal," said Bill. "What about me showin' you off at the Museum tonight? I'd like to see that phan-tas-ma-goria I read about in the *Gazette*. Sixty movin' figures, it says. Lord Nelson, Mary Queen of Scots, even the King of Prussia."

Where did Nicole get her energy? Amity wondered that evening. After Bill had handed Nance into the coach, climbed up to his seat, and driven off, Nicole gathered the children about her.

"Convey to them that I will fix their hair," she told Amity. "My father, he was what you call hairdresser. And my mother was lady's maid. So I know much about fashion."

Nicole didn't lack confidence, Amity decided, watching the girl shampoo the three heads, then comb and cut, effecting miracles with Nance's blunt scissors.

After the coiffures Nicole taught the children a dance. She placed them opposite one another, and took the fourth place herself.

> "Sur le pont d'Avignon
> L'on y passe, l'on y danse,"

she sang in a clear, lilting voice.

> "Sur le pont d'Avignon
> L'on y danse tout en rond."

Fascinated, the children watched her.

> "Les madames font comme ça."

Nicole dipped to the floor in a curtsey and helped Annie to hold out her brief skirt and bend her knees.

> "Les messieurs font comme ça."

She made a deep, formal bow and urged the boys to do the same. Then she held out her hands to the children on either side, motioned to all three to join hands, and skipped around in a circle with them until they tottered and fell down, weak with laughter. Soon she began the song again, gesturing to the children to sing with her. "Sur le pont d'Avignon—"

Amity suddenly remembered her father. He must be lonely in that stuffy room.

"Did I hear someone singing?" he asked. "In French?"

"Why don't you come and watch?" asked Amity. "The doctor didn't say you must stay in bed."

Darius Lyte closed his eyes. "Not tonight." Amity knew that tone of voice. If he wouldn't get up, she'd stay and visit with him.

Spinning flax for the Zion Duck and Sail Cloth Company was quite different from spinning at the low wheel in Gammer Foote's cottage. All day Amity stood in front of the whirring spindle, her fingers drawing a thread out from the bundle of tow, smoothing out lumps or slubs. All day Nicole must keep the wheel turning so that the spindle would twist the thread. All day Amity must take care that the thread be of uniform size. It must be firm and strong for sailcloth. She must not forget and draw the thread out too fine.

Everything in the vast, crowded loft was drab—the dark garments of the weavers and spinners, the gray frames of looms and wheels, and the lighter gray of tow. In all the room's unending twilight there was one spot of color—Nicole's scarlet dress.

When wheels and looms first started clacking, thumping, thwacking, and whirring all together, Amity thought the racket would deafen her. But she soon became accustomed to the noise, and could even talk with Nicole while they worked.

Others in the loft looked askance at them, for they did not understand French, and were suspicious that the two girls were talking about them. So Amity set about teaching Nicole English. She discovered that Nicole understood more than she would admit. "I can comprehend the English," she said, "but my tongue is French, and cannot say the English words."

Night after night the two girls walked wearily from

the loft, their backs aching and fingers raw from the tow and the wheel. As they made their way toward Link Alley the fresh air and exercise revived their spirits. Often Nicole would be skipping when they turned into the alley.

Tim's eager face was the first to greet Amity. When he was not waiting in the doorway, he was perched on a fence at the corner. After supper he helped Amity clear the table and wiped plates and cutlery. Then the three children gathered about Amity, clamoring, "A story. A story." Often Nicole joined them.

The favorite was the tale Amity had first told. Perhaps because it had the ring of truth, the story of the burning packet, the struggle across the mudflats, and the welcome at the marsh cottage never failed to delight them. Over and over again Tim begged her to tell it. And more often than not, when she finished, he would say, "I wish I could visit Gammer Foote."

On the mouse, Ebeneezer, Tim lavished a special love. He held the creature in his hands by the hour, crooning to it and stroking its head with a fingertip. The tiny beast soon spent more time in Tim's pocket than in its cage, an old tin lantern with scores of air holes punched in the sides, and a hinged opening that served as a door. On one point Amity was adamant. Ebeneezer must be locked in his cage at night. She had enough to worry about without a mouse scuttling across her bed.

Her first week's pay and the second, Amity turned over to Nance. When she proffered her third week's earnings, Nance took only half.

"Them slippers won't last another fortnight," she said.

Amity nodded. Nightly she cut pieces of cardboard to

fit inside them. If the makeshifts lasted through a day, she was lucky. But Doctor Barrus must be paid before she spent money on herself.

At the end of the following week Amity bought shoes, a stout pair suitable for a female who worked for wages. After that she would get some for Tim. He'd gone barefoot, gladly, after his boots had fallen to pieces. But the autumn would soon be upon them, and with it cold weather.

Autumn. Amity hardly dared to think of it. She had been living from day to day, hoping that each dawn would bring some improvement in their situation, that her father would soon regain the use of his arm and find a new post.

Tim was a worry to her, too. She saw him only in the early morning and evening. What he did all day or with whom he played besides the young Trasks, she had no idea. He was affecting rough mannerisms. He had a way of putting his hands on his hips, clearing his throat, and spitting onto the street. His speech was full of *his'n*'s and *her'n*'s and misplaced *them*'s.

One evening he pulled out from his shirt a large orange, gleaming in its perfection. "It's for you, Amity," he said.

Instantly she was suspicious. "Where did this come from?"

"I found it," he said, reddening.

"Are you sure?" She didn't want to accuse him of stealing.

He ducked his head and murmured, "Yes." But she was not convinced, and that night gave him a lecture on the evils of thieving.

The next afternoon as she was walking toward Link Alley she saw a farm wagon loaded with boxes of apples. On the side was printed Loammi Baldwin, Woburn.

The driver was hidden by a passing coach. Amity broke into a run. Perhaps it was Sam! But when she drew near, she saw that the man holding the reins was old. His hair was streaked with gray, and he wore the stolid look of a farmhand.

September passed. The air had a crisp tang that presaged autumn. Darius Lyte's arm was free of the splints, and he ventured out to the street. His color improved, as did his appetite. But his spirits did not. He was gloomy and taciturn. His right arm was weak, and his fingers stiff and clumsy.

Late one afternoon in early October Amity and Nicole left the Zion Company and started toward Link Alley. Far down Prince Street Amity saw a wagon with a load of apples. From this distance the name was illegible. Even if it were a Baldwin wagon, the same phlegmatic man was probably driving it. She didn't bother to point it out to Nicole. The two girls walked along briskly.

They were about to cross Middle Street when there was a loud cry of "Whoa!" from the lanes of moving carts and wagons. Two horses suddenly swerved out of line with a tossing of manes and jingle of harness, and came to a halt directly in front of the girls.

What did the driver think he was doing, handling his team so recklessly? Some teamsters thought they owned the roads. She'd give the fellow a piece of her mind.

Lifting her chin she looked up at the young man holding the reins, and the angry words died on her lips. She didn't need to read the name on the side of the wagon. There was no mistaking the shock of chestnut hair, the keen eyes, and the wide smile. Never in her life had she been happier to see anyone than she was to see Sam Baldwin.

8

Two Letters

The young man leaped to the sidewalk beside the girls.

"Mr. Baldwin!" Amity couldn't keep the happiness from her voice.

"Wherever have you been, Miss Lyte?" he demanded. "When I called at Mrs. Snow's, she said your father wasn't teaching there, and she had no idea where you were."

A shout came from the carts to the rear, their way blocked by Sam's wagon.

"Ho, there, up ahead! Get that team moving!"

"Why don't you and your friend ride along with me?" invited Sam. "I'm on my way to Mrs. Snow's to deliver these apples, and then I'll take you home."

Nicole was willing enough. She climbed up on the high seat like an agile monkey, her small face bright with excitement. Sam handed Amity up, then followed, while Amity made a hurried introduction. Slapping the reins on the horses' backs, Sam urged them forward. The wheels rattled on the cobbles, and the wagon turned into the stream of moving vehicles.

"I was afraid you had gone back to New York," said Sam. "Is everything all right?"

After Amity had recited her tale, he shook his head sympathetically. "That's too bad! You should have got in touch with me. My family could have helped out somehow."

"I did think of it," admitted Amity, carefully omitting the fact that her father had forbidden any such overture.

"Mrs. Snow's school is just a few streets from here. Are you sure you don't mind going there first? Uncle sends her a load of apples every year. The teamster is ill so I brought them in. Try one." He reached in back, picked up two beautiful red apples, and handed them to the girls.

Amity sank her teeth into the tart fruit. "What kind of apples are these?" she asked. It was a relief to talk about something so commonplace. She was still so excited over meeting Sam, she could hardly keep her thoughts straight.

"They're Baldwin apples, named after my uncle," said Sam. Laughter crinkled his eyes, and his grin was mischievous. "I told you he was an important man, didn't I?"

"He must be important to have an apple named after him," agreed Amity. Surely this was some joke Sam had made up to tease her. She didn't believe a word of it, but it was fun to let him think she did.

They left the business district and entered a residential section. The wagon turned a corner, and Amity recognized Green Street and the boarding school. A little more than three months ago she had entered it filled with hope. A good thing she had not known then what those mouths would bring.

Sam drew the horses to the side of the street and jumped down. "I'll not be more than a few minutes," he said, and took the path in long strides.

The front door was opened by the maid in the rose and green striped uniform. A moment later she was brushed aside as a young woman dashed out onto the porch and threw her arms about Sam's neck, kissing him soundly on both cheeks. "I am so glad to see you," she cried in a ringing voice, then drew him inside, while the maid followed after and closed the door.

Amity and Nicole looked at one another in amazement. "Veree strange, these American custom," said Nicole. "Does the grocer always go to the front door? And be welcomed so?"

"He's not a grocer," said Amity. She was as bewildered as Nicole. Sam had spoken as if he knew Mrs. Snow. But who was the young lady who had greeted him so effusively?

"Why does he drive a wagonload of apples if he is not a grocer?" demanded Nicole. "He is very handsome, your friend, no?"

Sam, handsome? Amity frowned. "I wouldn't call him handsome," she demurred. "His nose is too big, and his jaw juts out, and his eyebrows are too heavy."

"The young lady, she must think him handsome," said Nicole.

At that moment Sam came out the door and hurried down the path, his coat blowing open. "Mrs. Snow would like you to come in," he invited. "She has two letters for you."

Mystified, Amity followed, Nicole at her side. Who could be writing to her? She had not received a letter in her entire life.

Mrs. Snow welcomed the girls gravely. Amity responded politely, but her eyes flew over the little woman's head to the tall creature behind, dressed in the height of fashion. Her thick dark hair was piled in an untidy coronet. The pale eyes above her prominent nose regarded Amity with amused curiosity. In her arms she carried a tiny Maltese dog covered with long white fur.

"Sally, my dear, this is Miss Amity Lyte," said Mrs. Snow. "Miss Lyte, this is Miss Sally Thompson, the—" Her words were drowned out by a sharp burst of barking. For so small an animal the dog made a great racket. Amity thought she had heard the countess of something that sounded like Rumford, but her ears must have been playing her tricks. Countesses in the United States were few and far between, not likely to be found in a boarding school.

"Sally's family and the Baldwins have been friends for years," explained Mrs. Snow.

Very close friends, thought Amity, thinking of the enthusiastic welcome Sam had received. Disheveled and dusty after a day of spinning in the loft, sorely aware of her patched and mended dress, she had never felt more at a disadvantage. She tried to quell a rising resentment toward Sally Thompson.

"I wonder why I have not heard from your father," said Mrs. Snow, a hint of reproach in her tone. "Did he not understand that I wished to get in touch with him after making inquiries about a position?"

"Yes," said Amity carefully, "he understood, I am sure.

But an injury he suffered just after leaving here incapacitated him. In fact, he has still not recovered the full use of his arm."

"What a pity!" exclaimed Mrs. Snow. "I cannot help but feel responsible in a way. But let me give you your letters. One came several weeks ago, and the other but a few days back. I kept them, hoping that I might hear of your whereabouts." She put the two letters into Amity's hands. "We will excuse you if you wish to read them now."

Clearly Mrs. Snow was adept at managing people.

One of the letters was addressed in Mlle. Armand's delicate handwriting. Amity slid her finger under the wafer of sealing wax and carefully opened out the sheet. Was that a faint fragrance of verbena? The Frenchwoman hoped that Amity was pleased with her new life in Boston and that Mrs. Snow had engaged her as an assistant. Was Mr. Lyte having success in his teaching? She herself had taken a post as governess to the three daughters of Mr. Elijah Pratt of New Haven. With best wishes to the family, and affectionate regards to Amity, she closed with a request for her to write soon.

Sam had left the room and with the help of a man-servant was unloading the wagon. After Nicole replied to a few remarks from Mrs. Snow, Miss Thompson exclaimed, "*Ah, vous êtes parisienne!*" Then the two burst into a rapid torrent of French.

Amity fingered the second letter in bewilderment. The New York address had been scratched out, and the letter redirected in care of Mrs. Snow. In one corner, in spidery, shaky handwriting, was written: From K. L. Woods, Woburn, Massachusetts. Why was K. L. Woods writing to Amity? She broke the seal and spread out the sheet, putting the folded enclosure in her lap.

My dear Great-Niece,

I do not know if your father has told you of his family. Thirty years have passed since he left, and in that time he has not communicated with any member of our family, so I presume he has not wished to acknowledge former ties and has not apprised you of them.

Many changes have taken place. I will not dwell upon them or upon the sorrows and separations involved. I have reached the point where the beckoning of death's finger seems more friendly than frightening, but I am loath to relinquish my hold on our family home until I can give it into your hands.

My desire to make you my heir is not the senseless quirk of an old woman. I am aware that you have a brother, but he is your father's son, and may have as little regard for family ties as Darius. A woman has more feeling for a home.

With this in mind, I beg you to make the journey to Woburn and remain here with me, for I am lonely. Bring your brother, if you wish. Your father will make his own decision, as he ever has. He will be welcome if he cares to accompany you.

I enclose a draft to cover the expenses of the journey.

Your affectionate great-aunt,
Keziah Lyte Woods

The letter was dated September 1, 1805—over a month ago. Amity unfolded the enclosure with trembling fingers. It was a draft made out in her name, countersigned by Loammi Baldwin. The amount was for fifty dollars. Though fifty dollars was a fortune in terms of her weekly wage, she hardly noticed the sum. She took up the letter again and reread it slowly. Great-aunt Keziah. Aunt

Keziah. The name seemed to sing itself in her mind. Now they were not alone, she and her father and Tim. There was someone who belonged to them, someone who cared!

Her eyes began to brim. She brushed at the tears with her fingers. Miss Thompson bore Nicole off to her room to show her a water color just received from Paris. Amity found herself alone with Mrs. Snow.

"Have you received bad news?" the schoolmistress inquired.

"Not at all." Amity sniffed. "I could not imagine any better." Then she was telling Mrs. Snow about the letter. She had scarcely finished when the others returned.

"You are acquainted with many of the people in Woburn, are you not, Sam?" asked Mrs. Snow. "Do you know a Mrs. Woods, by any chance?"

"Mrs. Keziah Woods? Indeed I do. She lives just down the road from my uncle's house in the old Lyte place. The old Lyte place! Could you be related to her?"

"She's my father's aunt, and has invited us to visit."

"I remember Mrs. Woods. Who would not?" interposed Sally Thompson with a laugh that held a hint of malice.

"She may be a bit queer, but she's as kind as they come," said Sam stoutly. "I hope you're going to accept her invitation." His eyes were eager.

"I think we may," said Amity slowly, though she was already fearful of her father's reaction. "I'll have to find out when the coach leaves, and where," she continued.

"Coach!" scoffed Sam. "Who travels to Woburn by coach nowadays? The only civilized way to go is by the Middlesex Canal. Leave Boston in the morning and be there by noon. You'll have the safest, steadiest, prettiest ride of your life."

"Oh, Sam. You and your canal! You'd think there wasn't another in the world to hear you talk!" Sally Thompson shook a playful finger at him.

A gong sounded deep in the house and was followed by quick footsteps and girlish voices.

Amity rose. "We must be going," she said. "Thank you for your kindness."

"We'd be glad to have you join us for tea," said Mrs. Snow.

"Thank you, but my father will be anxious." Amity hurried out the door, Nicole and Sam following.

Jogging along on the wagon's high seat, Amity was beset by doubts. Though she held her great-aunt's letter in her hand as she would a talisman, a vision of her father's forbidding face clouded even the bright sunset throwing scarves of rose and gold across the sky.

Nicole was chattering gaily. "That Miss Thompson, she has lived in France. Did you see her gown, how chic? But her hair—*zut!* A pity she does not have the skill to dress it properly. If I could but get my fingers into it!"

Amity scarcely heard her, she was so tormented by doubts and fears. She wanted desperately to go to Wo- But her hair—*zut!* A pity she does not have the skill to sent was another matter. Woburn meant Loammi Baldwin, and Darius had shown such distaste for the man she couldn't imagine his going near the town. Moreover, what would Father say when he saw her riding with Loammi Baldwin's nephew?

As the lightened wagon bounced over the crooked streets, Amity struggled with another problem. How could she let Sam see the Trasks' dilapidated house? It couldn't be more of a contrast to Mrs. Snow's solid, imposing residence. And how could she introduce Sam to Bill and Nance? Good-hearted folk they were, but what would Sam think of their rough ways? Sam had declined an invitation to tea in order to take her home. He probably expected to be asked to stay for a meal. How could she invite him into the shabby kitchen with its heaps of dirty dishes?

They were nearing Link Alley. Sam was looking about with keen eyes. Amity came to an instant decision. "You can let us off here," she said. "It's just a step more, and we can walk."

Sam looked puzzled. "I'll be glad to take you to your door."

"We don't mind walking, do we?" Amity asked Nicole, hating herself for her cowardice.

"Oh, no," said Nicole. "To walk is good for the health."

"Well, if you're sure you want to get down here," said Sam dubiously, and slowed the team.

Just then a dark-green hackney coach with canary trim rumbled past. Bill Trask leaned out and shouted, "Hurry along, gals. The missus will be waitin' fer ye." He stared at Sam, gave Amity a broad wink, and added, "Bring yer young man if ye like. We can always water the soup!" The coach careened down the alley and turned into the shed.

There was no help for it. "Will you do us the honor of joining us for supper?" Amity asked stiffly. If only, for once, there would be a decent meal.

Sam bowed to her gravely. "The honor will be mine, ma'am," he said. Then he slapped the reins along the horses' backs and drove into Link Alley.

9

The Search

What a fool Amity had been to worry over senseless trifles; a minute later she was to meet with real trouble. Nance met her at the door, the twins clinging to her skirts.

"It's Tim," she said. "We can't find him. He's been gone most of the day." Her lips were pressed tightly together, and a frown creased her forehead.

"He's probably playing somewhere and forgot to come home," said Amity, trying to keep the tremor from her voice. Poor little Tim. Absorbed in Sam and her letters, she'd forgotten all about him.

"No," said Nance, "he's not just playin'. We've been huntin' for him since noontime. He's just—gone." She spread out her hands in a helpless gesture.

What could have happened to Tim? Had he been struck by a runaway horse? Or fallen down a well? Might he have been kidnaped? Some men made a business of stealing bright boys, passing them off as their own, and binding them over to merchants or cordwainers or smiths for a price. The man pocketed the money; the boy would have to work out a term of seven years or more.

"It's sure we won't find him jest standin' here," said Bill, "and night comin' on fast. We've got to look fer him. You"—he laid a hand on Sam's shoulder—"how well do ye know Boston?"

"I know the Common and Beacon Hill pretty well."

"Then you go over there. I'll take the waterfront. And you gals go down by the Zion Company. Ye'll be safe together."

They set off in three directions. Amity began to run, Nicole at her side. Fearfully they peered into alleys, looked in doorways. And they called, "Tim! Tim Lyte!" Their voices rang through the thickening dusk as they hurried to the Zion loft on the chance that Tim had gone there looking for them. When they arrived they searched around boxes and bales at the rear of the building, alerting the watchman.

"Who's there?" he challenged, brandishing a stick.

"Have you seen a little boy, six years old, about this tall?" Amity tried to keep the panic from her voice.

"Dozens of them. He's probably home by now." The man went on his way, his footfalls gradually fading away.

Nicole plucked at Amity's sleeve. "We should return and see if Tim is there now?"

"All right. But let's go back a different way and keep looking." Again they searched. Could he be behind that fence? In that empty hogshead? Under that broken-down shed? Prying and poking, the girls made their way toward Link Alley. There they met Darius Lyte stalking unsteadily along the road, the lines on his face etched deeper than ever.

Nance met them at the door, saying, "Not yet," to their unspoken question. The twins sat on the floor, close together. Noah looked at Amity with troubled eyes.

"Noah," said Amity, some sixth sense directing her, "can you tell me where Tim is?"

"I don't know," he said, beginning to cry. "He just ran."

"Ran where?" pursued Amity.

"Away," Noah sobbed, "away from that old man."

"What old man?" She'd keep on questioning him if it took all night.

"The one we stole the apples from."

"Stole apples? You? I'll learn you to steal." Nance dealt him a heavy blow.

Noah let out a howl. "We had to. The big boys made us. Said they'd gouge our eyes out if we didn't."

Amity was trembling. "Where did all this happen?"

"Down there," said Noah, pointing.

Down there proved to be near the market place, not far from Faneuil Hall. At this hour the streets were dark and deserted. The only traces of the produce-piled carts of an earlier hour were discarded cabbages and onions that squashed underfoot. Nance had brought a horn lantern with her. She swung it into empty stalls, peering here and there.

"Any luck?" Sam had seen them as he returned from Beacon Hill. They stood on what Noah claimed was the very spot where Tim had stolen the apple, been caught, and had run away. Noah pointed in the direction where Tim had run, but search as they might, they could find no sign of the small boy.

"All this for the sake of one apple," spluttered Sam.

"In Woburn a boy can find bushels of apples lying around on the ground, free for the asking."

Amity clenched her hands together. They were getting nowhere. She must use her head. If she were in Tim's place, lonely and frightened, where would she run? Back to the Trask house? Who was there but a grim father and a scolding Nance? Would he go to the Zion loft to find her? Not likely. He hardly knew its location, let alone how to find her in the huge building. There must be some other answer. She thought back to the day before. Could she find some clue there? The evening had gone along as usual, with Amity and Tim busy over dishes while Nicole got the young Trasks ready for bed. Then they had gathered around Amity for a story, and Tim had begged for the old tale about the shipwreck and Gammer and Gaffer Foote.

Of course! That was it! She sighed in satisfaction. "I know where we'll find him—at Daggart's Inn in Dock Square. He'll be looking for a ride to Connecticut on the stage that leaves in the morning."

Hope lent wings to her feet. When Nance and Nicole and the children straggled behind, Amity called over her shoulder, "Why don't you go back to the house?" She could not wait for them to keep up.

Sam took her hand and together they raced through the dark streets. Once she slipped on some rotten cabbage leaves, but Sam swept her along with his strong grasp. Here and there they passed a candlelit window, or a couple picking their way by lantern light, their shadows stretching before and behind them in swift motion.

They were halfway to the tavern when doubt knifed through her. Was this just a giddy idea? Had her mind accepted it as plausible because she was so excited by the day's events? She slowed her steps. "I'm beginning to wonder if he really is there."

"We'll never find out unless we look," said Sam, so matter-of-factly that she could do nothing but hurry along beside him. "That's where I'd go if I were Tim."

She could have hugged him. With renewed confidence she began to run again.

Lights flared around the entrance to Daggett's Inn. Men and women came and went through the wide doors. Bursts of song, snatches of conversation, and the clank of pewter tankards floated out each time the doors swung open.

"He'd surely not be inside," said Amity.

"Let's try the stable," Sam suggested. He led her through a narrow, slippery alley, rank with the smell of ordure. At its end loomed a shadowy stable. A snoring groom slumped in a chair at the entrance, a lighted lantern beside him.

Sam tiptoed toward him, picked up the lantern and beckoned to Amity. Together they entered the dark cavern. It was alive with sound—mice rustled in the grain; horses blew noisy breaths and shifted their hoofs with hollow thunder. They passed a row of stalls, each with its shifting rump or switching tail. At the far end was an empty cubicle. Amity's throat tightened. Surely Tim would be there. Sam lifted the lantern high, lighting each dark corner. But there were only cobwebs, a broken boot, and a rumpled straw hat.

Amity gestured the way to the other side of the stable

where harness and pitchforks ranged the walls. There was no place for a small boy to hide. For a few moments they stood stock still, and Amity felt a wave of despair. Perhaps Tim had not come here. Perhaps he was somewhere else in this huge city. He might even be trying to make his way to the marsh cottage on foot.

Sam walked to the center of the stable and gave a low whistle as he pointed to a corner. Had he found Tim? Amity looked where he pointed. With sinking heart she saw he had discovered, not a boy, but a narrow ladder, half hidden by a pile of hay. It led up through a black square into a loft.

Before Sam could set down the lantern Amity's hands were on the rungs, her feet lifting her upward. The rickety frame bent under her weight. Heedless, she climbed until she could thrust her head and shoulders through the opening. At first she could see nothing, but as her eyes became accustomed to the darkness, she could make out vast heaps of hay. There was no turning back now. She would have to look through every mound. She put an exploring hand on the rough planks and her fingers touched something warm. A rat? She drew back in terror. Then she heard a sigh, and a faint snuffle. Could it be? She reached out again and felt the shape of a small foot.

The next minute a shadowy form rose from the hay, and Tim's voice said tremulously, "Oh, Amity, I'm so glad you found me."

Then he was clinging to her, his wet cheek pressed close to hers, while the ladder teetered precariously.

10

On the Middlesex Canal

Whatever doubts Amity might have had about accepting Aunt Keziah's invitation had been forgotten as she searched for Tim. But within her grew a conviction that the sooner they left Boston the better.

All the powers of her imagination had not prepared her for the force of Darius Lyte's refusal. His eyes were somber the next morning when he read the letter. "I shall never return to Woburn," he stated flatly. He would stay at the Trasks' until he could find work. Or he would return to New York. His objections went on and on.

Every word strengthened her resolve. "You cannot stay here, Father. You must not expect the Trasks to care for you out of charity, and you have no work now. As for returning to New York, even if you could afford the journey, would you be any more successful in finding a position than you were three months ago? You must come with us, because I am going to Aunt Keziah, and I shall take Tim with me. I cannot leave you here."

He lifted his hand and started to speak again, but she

cut him short. "Father," she said wearily, "if I'm old enough to support us all, I'm old enough to make this decision."

His final protest came out weakly. "We cannot leave until we send her word as to our arrival."

"I wrote to her last night, Father. Sam Baldwin took the note and will deliver it today when he returns the wagon to his uncle." She didn't add that Sam, sensing her urgent need to get away, had offered to take them to Woburn that very day. He couldn't drive them later in the week since he had to return to his studies at Harvard.

"Aunt Keziah will expect us tomorrow noonday." Amity shot the final bolt and left her father quivering. She was shaking as she left the room, saying to herself, "If I'm capable of supporting us all by spinning, I'm capable enough to make this decision."

She was almost crying. Perhaps there was some sinister reason why her father refused to return to Woburn. Had he committed some crime? Her mind recoiled from the thought. Surely he was incapable of such a thing.

She brushed her eyes with the back of her hand. Tears showed weakness, and that was one thing she could not afford. One little crack in the armor of her self-sufficiency and her father might think of effective ways to break down her determination.

There was also the problem of Nicole. Amity had grown fond of the gay French girl. Should she invite her to go with them?

Before Amity broached the subject, Nicole plunged in with characteristic abruptness. "Amité," she said, throwing her arms around the older girl, "I shall be *desolée* to be part from you. But you must go to your *tante*, and I must remain here to wait for *mon oncle*. Who can tell, he might return to Boston tomorrow?"

"Perhaps you could remain at the Zion Company," said Amity.

"That will not be *necessaire*. In the next street there is a *coiffeur*, a man who dresses the hair. He would have me assist with shampoos and hair cuttings. And Mme. Trask has said I may remain here." So it was settled.

Amity informed the manager of the Zion Company that he could hire another decayed gentlewoman, her fortunes having taken an upward turn. She took Aunt Keziah's draft to a merchant recommended by Sam Baldwin, and obtained the money. All the way back to Link Alley she was tempted by the shop windows she passed. Come buy a new jacket for Tim. Here is a fine suit for your father. And oh, the gowns—of calico, dimity, lawn, and muslin! She was on the point of buying one, but checked herself. How could she explain to Aunt Keziah that she had spent her traveling money on new clothes? They would present themselves in their worn, threadbare garments, which would at least be clean. She spent her last afternoon in Boston washing, ironing, and mending. Even then she and Tim would wear clothing borrowed from the Trasks' scant store.

When Bill came home that evening, he carried a tall beaver hat, its crown encircled by a jaunty red band. With a flourish he presented it to Darius Lyte. "A gent bound for England left it in my coach today. He's well down the harbor now, and there's nary a chance of my givin' it back. Here's a good headgear for Mr. Lyte, sez I. There's no one needs it more."

Darius flinched and half raised his hand in a gesture of rejection. Something in Bill Trask's face stopped him. His hand dropped, and he said, "Very kind of you, I'm sure." He put the hat on his head, where it wobbled uncertainly, being a size small. "How does it look?" he asked.

"Very handsome," Amity said before anyone could voice a criticism. Bill beamed and Nance nodded in approval. Tim and the twins clapped their hands. Everyone was pleased that Darius Lyte would journey to Woburn properly hatted.

When the three Lytes were about to climb into the hackney coach the next morning, the twins solemnly handed Tim the lantern cage. Inside were Ebeneezer and a large crust of bread.

"You take him," said Noah. "Twins is never lonely. But you ain't got a soul to play with."

Nance caught Amity in her stout arms. "Seems as though we've got used to you folks," she said, wiping her eyes. "We won't know how to get along without you."

Amity felt a swift and surprising rush of affection. She would miss Bill and Nance, their scolding and chaffing, their warmth and generosity.

Then Bill was slapping the reins over Jezebel's back, and the coach jolted down the lane and out into the brisk morning traffic. Tim held fast to the lantern cage. He put his small face close to it, murmuring, "Don't be afraid, Ebeneezer. I'll take care of you."

Less than an hour later they arrived at the Beachum Landing in Charlestown. Porters wheeled hand trucks loaded with boxes and bales. Carts were lined up to take cargo from freight boats to nearby warehouses, and wagons rolled toward the Charles River bridge. Carriages and gigs discharged their passengers, the gentlemen in tailed coats, the ladies in pelisses or capes. Mingling with them were country folk, the men in rough, lumpy tweeds, the women in calicoes and homespuns.

The nearby Bunker Hill Tavern was doing a brisk business, despite the early hour. Drivers came down the walk wiping their mouths with burly fists. Men and women passengers hurried through the wide doors toward the gaudily painted boat that lay beside the wharf.

"Ye'd best be gettin' aboard if ye want a seat. Looks summat crowded today." Bill jumped down from his seat to open the coach door. As he helped her out, Amity pressed a bill into his hand. He flushed, and made a move to return it. "I could no more take money from ye than from my own sister," he protested. "Gwan, take it back."

"It's part of the money for our traveling expenses," said Amity.

"Well, in that case—" said Bill with a grin, and pocketed the money. Waving an arm at the shouting drivers lined up in back of him to discharge their passengers, he called out, "Don't get het up, I'm goin'." And he was off.

Holding fast to her father's arm with one hand, and Tim's fingers with the other, Amity made her way through the surging crowd to the passenger agent's box. A thin, sallow-faced man was taking in money and dealing out pasteboard squares. Behind him a red-faced official urged him to hurry. Posted over the window was a flyer, announcing, *The* George Washington, *30 tons, passenger service from Charleston to Chelmsford 75c Joseph Wardwell, Commander.*

"Where you going, Miss?" asked the man impatiently.

"To Woburn."

"Which stop? Woburn Village or Newbridge?"

Puzzled, Amity was silent.

"Newbridge," came her father's voice.

The man shoved out three tickets. "That'll be a dollar and a quarter. Fifty cents each, and half fare for the boy."

Then they could board the long, narrow boat with *George Washington* painted in large black letters on its red wale, just above the white strip that marked the water line of the black hull. The quarter railing was bright red, the posts a light blue, and the seats and interior a brilliant orange. It looked more like a circus barge than a passenger boat.

Beside the rail on the afterdeck there was just room for three. Amity had started toward the empty space when her father said, "It's too public out here. I'm going into the cabin."

"But it's such a beautiful day!" Amity lifted her head in the sunlight, trying to take in all together the white puffs of cloud in the deep blue October sky, the long ribbon of water stretching ahead toward the marshes that bordered the Mystic River, and the jumble of boats and rafts moving through the basin.

"Stay out here if you wish. I'm going inside." Darius Lyte's words were cut short by the loud blare of a bugle. The red-faced man emerged from the booth and hurried across the gangplank.

"Look, Amity, they're hitching up the team." Tim rested the lantern on a vacant seat and pointed to a pair of horses, hitched tandem, that thundered across the dock and came to a halt a little ahead of the *Washington's* bow. A burly hand hooked the singletree to the towrope, and the driver mounted.

The horn sounded again, so close that Amity jumped. The red-faced man was standing on the deck nearby, the bugle in his hand. "All aboard!" he bawled.

Three men ran across the gangplank, carpetbags swinging. Two sailors pulled the plank smartly inboard, and a pair of deckhands cast off the tie ropes. The driver urged the horses forward to take up the slack of the towrope.

Another blast of the horn, and a shout from the captain, "Get them moving, boy!" The driver brought his whip across the horses' backs. They plunged against the harness, their shoulders bulging and hoofs digging calked shoes into the planks. The boat trembled. The steersman braced himself, leaning against his long, twenty-foot oar. The water at the stern began to ripple; the furrow split into a wake. The dock slid past astern, its knots of workmen and bystanders shouting and waving.

Soon the packet moved smoothly and silently. It seemed strange to be traveling with no jangle of harness, no creaking of springs or rattling of wheels. The horses, well ahead of the boat and tugging on the eighty-foot rope, moved without sound. Only the crack of the driver's whip floated back in the clear morning air. Soon they were skirting the Mystic River, its bulrushes and reeds waving in the brisk breeze. Across the river a red brick house shone bright against marsh grasses.

Some of the passengers climbed onto the deck that

roofed the cabin. Tim tugged at Amity's hand. "Can I go up there?" he begged.

The upper deck appeared perfectly safe. A few gentlemen strolled back and forth on the narrow space. One with a round bald head and hooked nose was in deep conversation with a tall, slender young man with a sharp face and smooth, light hair.

"Be careful not to go near the edge," warned Amity. She took the lantern cage and watched Tim clamber up the steps. She would have liked to go with him, but there were no women in the group, and she felt diffident about being the only one. She found a seat where she could watch him, put the cage under it, and sank back.

Slowly her anxiety drained away. Her eyes traveled back along the canal toward the smoky pall that hung over Boston, then ahead into the bright day, gay with flashes of autumn color. Was the journey symbolic of her life? Was she leaving trouble and discouragement behind, entering a new world of light and hope? It was good to think so.

Her thoughts flew ahead to Aunt Keziah. She envisioned her as another Gammer Foote, in a cottage as charming and simple as the one beside the Connecticut marsh. Poor Aunt Keziah was probably bent and weary and in need of a niece's help. Amity would brush the hearth, and cook, and wash tubs of linen. What if her aunt were a bit queer as Sally Thompson had intimated? Amity would love her all the more for her eccentricities.

From ahead came the cry of the driver. "Bridge!"

At the packet's stern the steersman echoed, "Low bridge!"

Amity hardly heard their voices and took little notice

of the passengers descending from the upper deck. Then she saw that the boat was approaching a wooden bridge, across which carts and wagons rumbled. On its rail three boys perched, shouting and pointing toward the packet.

In one frantic glance she saw Tim, a tiny figure in the middle of the upper deck, gazing toward the rear, his back to the danger. She must get to him and bring him off the deck before the boat shot under the bridge and he was struck by the heavy timbers.

She tried to shout, but the breeze blew her words away. In one bound she was up and racing for the steps. But as she put her foot on the first stair a man hurtled past and up on the deck. He leaped to Tim's side, caught hold of his hand, and pulled him along with such speed that Tim fairly sailed through the air. Not a moment too soon they reached the edge of the deck and jumped, as the boat slid under the moss-covered timbers of the bridge. Overhead a horse's hoofs pounded, sending down sand and gravel through the cracks.

Amity walked shakily to where Tim stood, white-faced and trembling. The tall young man drew his hand across his forehead. "That was close," he said.

"I'm most grateful to you," said Amity. "I don't know what I'd do if anything should happen to my brother." She pressed Tim close to her side.

"It isn't every day I get a chance to be of service to a charming young lady," he said, bowing. Then he added, "Luke Fenwick's my name."

His look of admiration was disarming. "I'm Amity Lyte," she said, "and this is my brother Timothy." She couldn't help returning his smile.

"Are you going all the way along the canal—I hope?" he asked. There was nothing shy about him.

"Just to Newbridge," she said, and couldn't resist adding, "where my aunt lives." To have an aunt was new and exciting. She gave Tim's shoulder a squeeze.

"She must be a rather special aunt," commented Luke.

Amity drew back. There was no harm in his remark. Why, then, did she feel a certain wariness?

"We've never seen her, but we know she's nice because she's going to give her house to Amity," Tim said.

"Tim," she reproved, "we don't talk about our private affairs to strangers."

"Surely you don't consider me a stranger, Miss Lyte, after—" Luke Fenwick paused and looked meaningfully at the upper deck.

What was the matter with her? Tim should not have spoken out, but what he had said was true. And Luke Fenwick had saved Tim from possible injury. The least she could do to show her gratitude was to be friendly.

"I didn't know I was rescuing the brother of an heiress," Luke continued. Had his eyes a new sparkle?

She cut him short. "I'm certainly not that. Aunt Keziah just needs someone to look after her and take care of her cottage."

If he was disappointed, he made a quick recovery. "Even a small place may become valuable. It depends on where it is. When the canal was cut through, property values rose all along its route. That's why I'm here. I'm looking for land that will be a good investment for Mr. Dix." He glanced toward the hook-nosed man, now in deep conversation with Captain Wardwell. "They don't come any smarter than Strobo Dix," he said. Excepting Luke Fenwick, his smile suggested.

A freight boat proceeding ponderously ahead of the packet swerved into midstream. Its team halted, the towline went slack and the *Washington's* team passed over it, while the freight boat's men waved.

"Is that another bridge?" asked Tim, pulling at Amity's arm. Her eye followed his pointing finger. Crossing the Mystic River a full ten feet above its surface, the canal continued on, a ribbon of steel gray water borne in a gigantic trough supported by two stone abutments and three stone piers. Sam Baldwin had been telling the truth, after all.

"That's called an aqueduct," said Luke.

"I've heard about them," Amity said. The packet slid into the dark entrance like a shuttle into the narrow tunnel of a loom's separated warp. Thin bands of sunlight pierced the gloom, and the horses' hoofs made a hollow sound. She shivered. It seemed strange to pass over a river on a man-made stream.

Then they were out in the sunlight again, and Tim urged her to look forward once more. "What's that up ahead?"

A wooden structure rose before them, a long, narrow box with a high timbered wall at its farther end.

"Haven't you ever seen a lock before?" asked Luke.

Captain Wardwell blew a loud blast on his horn. The *Washington* drew up close to the opening where massive gates swung wide. The lock keeper was waiting for them, and the yawning gateway swung shut behind them. Water spilled from the level above into the gigantic wooden box, lifting the packet as easily as if it were a toy. Then they were at the top, and the lock gates were opened. The horses moved ahead to take up the slack, and the boat moved into the upper level of the canal.

"This canal is going to make a lot of money for some lucky people," said Luke. "I wish I'd thought of the idea."

"It must have taken a lot of work to build," said Amity. A picture of Sam flashed in her mind, a younger Sam, freckle-faced and eager, tagging after a dignified gentleman carrying rolls of plans and issuing orders to workmen.

The *Washington* continued its even progress as the driver kept the horses at a steady four miles an hour. If the packet went faster than that, the wash would cut into the bank and Captain Wardwell would have to pay a fine, Luke said.

Occasionally they passed a freight barge, or rafts of logs floating down from New Hampshire. The countryside unfolded on either side. Here were fields of pale brown stubble, there a stand of autumn rye, springlike in its tender green, then a village, where pumpkins and squash made orange mounds beside barns.

Tim held the caged mouse near the rail. "Ebeneezer likes to see where we're going," he told Amity.

There was another lock, and then the canal skirted a large lake so close that Amity felt as if they were floating on its surface. They passed through another lock, and still another, this one of great stone blocks. Beyond was a tree-fringed pond with a small island in the center where a pavilion stood in a grove of trees. Beside the canal was a spacious tavern.

"This is Horn Pond," said Luke Fenwick. "Parties come out here from Boston in the summertime to listen to the band that plays in the pavilion, and take their meals on the island. It's a gay place."

Three locks at the pond lifted them still higher, and the boat drew up at a landing. The captain called out, "Woburn Village." He looked over his shoulder at Amity and said, "We'll stop at Newbridge next."

Were they almost there? The morning had flown by. Poor Father must think she had completely abandoned him. Dipping a curtsey to Luke, she said, "It's time for me to join my father. Thank you for your help."

She held out her hand, and as he bent over it he said, "You've made a tedious trip pass pleasantly."

"I enjoyed it too," she said. Then realizing that he was still holding her hand, she pulled away abruptly, and went to the cabin.

At first she did not see her father and wondered for a panicky moment if he had made good his vow never to step foot in Woburn again. But then she saw him, slouched in a corner, a newspaper covering his upper half. There was no mistaking those long legs, or the hat with its red band on the seat beside him.

"We're nearly at Newbridge," she said.

The newspaper was lowered and his eyes appeared. But he did not rise until the packet had shuddered to a halt. And when he left the packet he walked onto the landing like a man in a trance.

11

The Vine-covered Door

Stalking ahead, looking neither to right nor left, Darius Lyte led the way through Newbridge back toward Woburn Village. His brown coat with its black velvet collar was tightly buttoned despite the sun's warmth. On his head the beaver hat with its red riband sat slightly askew. Amity had to hurry to keep up with his long steps. Tim was half running, the lantern cage swinging from his hand. The few people on the streets eyed the trio with curiosity.

Amity darted quick looks from side to side, noting the frame houses with neat gardens lining their paths. She longed to ask her father a hundred questions. How far was it to Aunt Keziah's house? What does she look like? Are you fond of her? She felt with increasing intensity the need to know why her father had left Woburn.

Now was not the time to ask, she knew. Would there ever be a right time, a time when she would learn why he had gone away from this seemingly peaceful village?

The road roughly paralleled the canal. On their right

stood a large square mansion. As they drew near, Darius Lyte crossed to the left side of the road, increasing his speed. Then there was a bridge that spanned the canal. Ahead were apple orchards, some of the trees bowed with crimson fruit. Soon they must arrive at Aunt Keziah's. Amity searched for the small frame house she had pictured as belonging to her aunt. Only one dwelling met her eye. Yellow and white, it was set well back from the road facing the canal, with a balustraded roof topping three stately stories. A long two-storied section extended at the rear, its roof line broken by the squat bulk of a massive chimney.

They must still have a considerable distance to go. It's somewhere beyond the yellow house, thought Amity. She strained for a sight of a modest, one-story, weather-beaten place with perhaps a bent figure outside waiting for them.

They drew abreast of the yellow house. Darius Lyte turned into the broad pathway and with a glance over his shoulder, said, "Well, here we are."

Amity stared along the leaf-strewn walk. Rowan trees bordered it, their bright red-orange berries and golden leaves shining brilliantly. Cedar waxwings darted among the trees, feasting on the berry clusters. She lifted her eyes to the house. Its yellow clapboards were bordered with white quoins and a cornice. A white pediment surmounted each window, and the doorway was framed by fluted pilasters topped with carved pineapples. In the noonday hush the house had an air of welcome and serenity.

Amity stood rooted, unbelieving as her eyes swept the stately charm of the house. She must be dreaming. It couldn't be true that this beautiful place was Aunt Keziah's and would one day be her own!

Only when her gaze fastened on the front door did she notice that vines had crept across its panels and were reaching up to the fanlight. Her eyes flew to the windows. Across each pane of glass, tendrils had woven a leafy shutter. She felt a chill as if a cloud had passed overhead. But the sun shone noon-high in a clear sky. Why was she shivering? Did past sorrows hover here?

Her voice came out in a near sob. "There must be some mistake, Father. No one is living here."

Poor man, he had been through so many trials, it was no wonder he had forgotten what his family home looked like. She turned to retrace her way down the path, when Tim, beside her, gave a whimper of fatigue. She turned to see if her father was following.

Darius Lyte had stopped several paces behind her, and was looking across the broad lawn toward a clump of cedars. A figure stepped out from behind the corner of the house, a tall spare woman with snowy white hair. The blue and violet silk of her gown shimmered like a pigeon's wing. She picked up the edges of her apron and flapped its white folds toward the cedars.

"Shoo!" she hissed. Then, in a shaking voice she said, "Drat you, cat! Go away! Scat!"

She let go of her apron and clapped her hands together. The sound cracked across the noonday hush. Some movement must have caught her eye, for she turned and stopped in the middle of a clap. She stood with her hands poised in midair, while an orange and white cat slithered from under the cedar branches and streaked across the lawn to the road. She did not even glance in its direction. She had eyes only for the group on the front walk.

With quick, jerky steps she hurried toward the gaunt man, her arms outstretched. For a brief moment Darius Lyte's years dropped away. His face was that of a young man as he went to meet her.

"Darius," she faltered, "oh, Darius—I'd hardly dared to hope—"

Then she lifted her face to his, her blue eyes brimming, and Darius Lyte swept her to him in a close embrace.

"Aunt Keziah," he said hoarsely, "we've come home."

12

The Lyte Homestead

Amity was enveloped in a glow that rivaled the Indian summer for sheer magic. Enchantment seemed to flow from Aunt Keziah. Amity loved her at once. Her blue eyes looked deep into Amity's as she said in her dry voice, "My dear, to think that I've had a great-niece such as you all these years and not been able to enjoy her!"

Her wrinkled hand stroked Tim's dark hair. "This boy's the very spit and image of his father," she observed fondly. Then she took her nephew's arm and led the way across the lawn, her long silk gown whispering over the grass. Tim's dark eyes rolled up, signaling to Amity. Here was the old lady Sam Baldwin had spoken of, the one who couldn't bear to have cats preying on her birds!

They turned the corner of the house and faced a long ell. The sun shone full upon a flower-filled courtyard and on windows curtained in crisp white. The door stood open, and on the threshold stood Bessie, a roly-poly little woman with silver braids wound around her head. Her plump hands dusted, scrubbed, ironed, cooked, and cleaned with a devotion that forty years of service in the Lyte household had not sapped. Her round face with its button nose and twinkling brown eyes was ever ready with a smile for her beloved family.

In the days that followed Amity had hours of freedom to wander with Tim through field and orchard, or to stroll along the canal path, scurrying out of the way of tow horses when barges, packets, or rafts or logs floated past. They listened to the winding notes of horns blowing for the Woburn or Newbridge landings.

Amity delighted in Bessie's bountiful meals, lusciously concocted and served on prized Lowestoft china. She basked in the sunlit garden, listening to lilting birdsong. And at the day's end she rested between smooth sheets in a room of her own.

Tim was happiest exploring the barn. He sat for hours on an old saddle, pretending he was riding a horse. Ebeneezer went everywhere with him, snug in a pocket or perched on his shoulder. The mouse was as welcome as its master, for as a boy Darius had brought home wild creatures for pets. Now and then Tim came to Amity, his face woebegone. "I wish I had someone besides Ebeneezer to play with," he said wistfully. "I miss Noah and Annie."

"You'll find some playmates soon," she said comfortingly. But a few minutes later she forgot his words.

The dressmaker came, bearing lengths of lawn, muslin, batiste, and mull. Only the filmiest, lightest materials were worn, she declared, even in the fall and winter months. After days of fittings, Amity had three new gowns—one of creamy white, one a pale lavender, the third a soft fawn—and a sage-green velvet spencer that complemented them all. Then the seamstress made a party gown of pale-green satin, and a reseda-green pelisse with a black velvet border and a bonnet with ostrich tips to match.

The tailor brought samples of cashmere and serge, and measured Darius Lyte for two new suits, and Timothy as well.

Freed from responsibility, Amity felt as limp—and as purposeless—as a petal dropping from one of the late damask roses.

She wandered aimlessly through the house. The part that Aunt Keziah lived in was the old homestead built generations ago, and Amity loved the worn sills, the uneven floorboards, and small paned windows. But the great square three-story structure on the front that her grandfather had built in 1750 held a special fascination. Again and again she begged the key from Aunt Keziah, and every time she unlocked the door connecting the two parts of the house, her heart beat faster. The storehouse of family treasures mystified and challenged her. Sometimes when she went into a room she felt that ghostly voices had just ceased speaking, and sometimes she could almost feel the brush of unseen hands on hers.

The beauty of the rooms never failed to thrill her—the carved woodwork, the rich colors of the hangings, the graceful curves of the furniture. She walked dreamily through parlor, study, music and dining rooms, mounted the wide staircase, her hand trailing on the mahogany rail, and paused in each of the eight bedrooms, listening with an inward ear for whatever secret the highboys, the tilt-top tables, the brass candlesticks might tell.

Once she tried to open the great front door, but found it locked. She would have liked to fling it wide and look through the arched rowan trees to the canal. She said as much to Aunt Keziah, but a closed expression came over the parchment face. "That door has been locked for thirty years," Aunt Keziah said with finality, and something in her tone forbade questioning.

Shadowy avenues into the past opened a crack at a time. Sometimes echoes of past happiness filled the house, like the perfume of the potpourri in the bowl on the spinet piano. One evening they were all sitting around the fire that flicked orange lights over the sitting room. Bessie, her needles clicking in a sock for Tim, stopped her rocking and chuckled.

"Will you ever forget, Miss Keziah, the time Master Darius brought his pet rooster into the kitchen, and the pesky bird flew into the dining room where your mother and father were entertaining the magistrate? And how the cock lit on the table and pecked at the bread on the plates, as cool as if he was in his own pen?"

Aunt Keziah looked up from her embroidery frame and laughed. Tim, curled up on the sofa beside Amity, giggled. From the wing chair in a dark corner a voice said, with a faint undertone of mirth, "You're wrong, Bessie."

Amity started. Could that be her father?

"The cock didn't eat bread. He was far more daring. There was fresh corn that night, and the cock perched on the magistrate's shoulder and helped himself to the ear that His Honor had just lifted to his lips."

Amity held her breath. Her father had not spoken so lightly in years. She glanced at Aunt Keziah, but there was no break in the brittle voice that remarked, "That cock thought he was a human being masquerading in comb and wattles." Only the tremor of her hand, holding a needle above a design of colored wools, betrayed agitation.

Darius Lyte said no more than his usual "Good night" before he went up the staircase, candle in hand. But hardly had his bedroom door shut with a soft click when Bessie burst out, "Did you hear Mister Darius?"

Aunt Keziah cut her short. "Bessie, nothing is so destructive to family harmony as the discussion of one member by the others." Then she softened. "We are both devoted to him, Bessie, but we must let him be. He will never come to rights with himself and others if he has two old women hovering over him."

Days passed. Darius Lyte took to walking through the fields. Gradually he regained the full use of his arm. He entered into brief conversations, and commented on the crimson, rust, and scarlet of the oak leaves. Amity had begun to hope that he had left behind his former fears when one dreadful morning the door into the past opened to let in bitter memories.

Bessie had made a breakfast of crisp links of sausage and pancakes filled with cubes of apple. Darius asked for a second serving, and observed, "You're an even better cook than I remember, Bessie! What is your secret?"

"It's that new-fangled cooking arrangement your aunt bought for me. When I used the old open fireplace, I cooked my own self nearly as much as the food. But this box contraption invented by Count Rumford keeps the fire in one place, so it heats the pots and pans but not the cook." She was about to go on, but at a warning frown from Aunt Keziah, screwed her mouth tight shut and hurried into the kitchen.

Darius was scowling fiercely. "Rumford," he muttered. "Must I be reminded of that man even now?"

Aunt Keziah took a deep breath. "Ben Thompson is on the other side of the ocean and not likely to return. His Rumford stoves are a great convenience. I saw no point in penalizing Bessie because of our personal feelings. The sooner you forget what happened between you two, the better."

"Forget the man who betrayed his country?" Darius glowered at the faces around the table, then stalked out of the room.

Amity's mind buzzed with questions. What in her father's past distracted him when certain names were mentioned? First Loammi Baldwin, and now Count Rumford, or Benjamin Thompson. Sally Thompson was the young woman she had met at Mrs. Snow's. Wasn't she the Countess of something? Of course, it had been Rumford, although that silly dog had all but deafened her with its yapping. She was probably Benjamin Thompson's daughter. But how could the child of a traitor be a close friend of Colonel Baldwin, who had led a regiment in the Continental Army? Amity longed to ask about many things. Why had Darius Lyte left home? And why was the big front door never opened?

In a day or two Darius's moodiness vanished. Amity could feel hope rising in her like the leaven in Bessie's fragrant loaves of bread. If her father could be freed from his inward torment he might in time resume his portrait painting.

13

The Bible Box

One evening Aunt Keziah announced, "I am expecting a visitor, a neighbor and friend for sixty years. I am sure he will be glad to see you."

Darius Lyte rose swiftly to his feet. "You don't mean—" he began.

"Colonel Baldwin is in the habit of calling on me often. I see no reason why he should change his custom." Aunt Keziah's tone was even. "We have business to transact."

"I have no wish to see Loammi Baldwin this evening or any other time," said Darius. He picked up a candle holder and went upstairs.

"But, Darius—" his aunt protested. The sound of the door closing was his only answer. She sighed deeply. "Dear me, one would think I'd used up all my tears long ago," she said, and brushed her fingers across her cheek.

Loammi Baldwin. Amity's pulse quickened. What was he like, this Colonel of the Revolution, County Sheriff, Representative to the General Court, Special Justice, and

most important of all, in Sam's eyes, Superintendent of
the Middlesex Canal? And then there was Sam's joke
about the apple.

The tall case clock was striking eight when Bessie
bustled to answer a knock on the door, and a man stepped
into the room. He was solidly built and of no more than
middle height, but there was such dignity in the set of
his head and his erect bearing that he seemed tall. His
face was calm, with strong features—wide-set gray eyes
under neat brows, an aquiline nose, and a firm mouth.
For all his honors and offices he showed no sign of
pomposity.

He bowed over Aunt Keziah's hand. "My dear," he
said, "I must beg your forgiveness for not coming earlier
to welcome your family. But my mind has been flying
like the chariots of Amminadib to keep pace with the
various works people would have me do—and I have been
hard put to get from Medford to Saco and back to Boston
as rapidly as they desire."

"What are you up to now, another canal?" asked
Keziah.

"There's the Medford Branch Canal uniting the Middlesex Canal with the Mystic River. And the new India
Wharf in Boston that Mr. Bulfinch designed and I must
execute, and a canal in Maine with a town some folk
insist on naming after me." He shrugged his shoulders,
chuckling, then took a few steps toward Amity, both
hands outstretched. "So this is the young lady who
endured shipwreck and losses with such courage? Samuel
was so lavish in his praise of you that I wondered how
much I could believe."

Amity's reserve melted. How could she feel stiff or

self-conscious with this man? "I was puzzled too," she returned. "Your nephew made you sound like the most famous man in the world. He said there were even apples named after you."

The corners of Loammi Baldwin's mouth turned upward, and the twinkle in his eyes grew brighter. Aunt Keziah gave her dry, husky laugh, and Bessie burst forth in a peal of merriment.

"At heart I'm just a simple country squire who likes to dig ditches and grow apples," said Colonel Baldwin, "and if I'm to be remembered by future generations, I'd choose to be known for my work on the Middlesex Canal and the Baldwin apple."

Amity felt her cheeks burning. When would she learn to hold her tongue, and to think before she spoke?

Colonel Baldwin's laugh dissolved her embarrassment. "I don't wonder that you thought Sam was joking. He is full of mischief, and all my children tease me about the Baldwin apple."

Bessie lifted her face earnestly. "These young folks don't know how important apples are, especially the good firm kind that keep all winter long."

"Sit down, Loammi, and tell Amity your apple story. You can take time for that." Aunt Keziah tapped the Windsor chair next to her with a thimbled finger. The Colonel lifted the tails of his coat and sat down.

"One autumn day about twelve years ago I was surveying for the canal a bit north of here," he said, "when I saw a flock of woodpeckers around a wild apple tree. I figured that woodpeckers are smart birds, so I picked an apple and ate it. I'd never sunk my teeth into a juicier, tarter apple. I took a bagful home to my dear wife, and she made some of them into a pie. What a pie that was! She stored the rest of the apples in the fruit cellar. In the spring she went for them and they were near as firm then as the day I picked them. So I betook myself to that tree and cut scions from it and grafted them onto trees in my orchard. Each spring I cut more scions from the ones I had started until now half the county is enjoying those apples." He leaned back in his chair and stretched his legs out to the fire.

"Tell how it was named after you, Loammi," urged Aunt Keziah.

"Oh, that." Colonel Baldwin waved his hand in protest, but it was clear he was pleased. "I called it the wood-pecker apple. But at a meeting of the Horticultural Society somebody proposed that it be called the Baldwin. And so it is."

For a few minutes they sat in silence while the fire's low flames throbbed. Then Aunt Keziah rose. "If you'll come this way, we'll take care of our business. Bring a candle and light the way for us, Amity."

Aunt Keziah unlocked the heavy door that separated the two parts of the house, and led them through the hallway, past the balustraded staircase, and into the front parlor. Going to each window in turn, she pulled hinged wooden shutters across the panes. Then she moved to the fireplace, and motioned Amity to set the candle on the carved mantel. While Aunt Keziah fumbled in her pocket, Amity looked at the portrait above the chimney piece. Candlelight shone on the narrow face with its sensitive mouth and dark eyes. She wished she might have known her great-grandfather.

Aunt Keziah drew a key out of her pocket and reached up to grasp one corner of the portrait. It swung out, revealing a small door. A twist of the key, a squeak of the lock, and her aunt was saying, "Reach in and lift out the box, Amity. I declare, I'm getting more stiff with each day."

The wooden box was intricately carved and worn smooth by countless hands. "It's the Bible box the first Lyte brought with him to this country," explained Aunt Keziah. "The Bible fell apart long since, and I couldn't think of a better place to keep our funds than in the box. Set it on the table, Niece. And put the light alongside, so I can read Loammi's bill."

The colonel brought a sheet of paper from his pocket. "Your expenses have been heavier this month, Keziah, but that's understandable with your increased family." He looked toward Amity. "Some years ago I persuaded your aunt to buy some of my surplus produce rather than keep her own cow and chickens and garden."

"I'm glad to help a neighbor by giving him my trade," said Aunt Keziah graciously.

"Don't think I'm not grateful," said the Colonel seriously.

Aunt Keziah produced a smaller key, fitted it into the ornate lock, and lifted the lid. Within were piles of currency. She lifted a banknote, held it to the candle, and peered at the figure. Amity leaned forward to look at the money. It was different from the notes she had handled in Boston. Where had she seen currency like this? A faint recollection stirred in her mind. She was moving closer to the box when the colonel stepped in front of her, blocking her view. "Seventy-five dollars should be about right, Keziah," he said. "That will take care of your bill and give you about fifty to carry you until next time."

"Yes, I'll need that much." She handed him the bank-note which he stuffed into his pocket.

"I'll give you your receipt and change in the other room." The Colonel closed the lid abruptly, turned the key, handed it to Keziah, and lifted the box to the cup-board and locked it. A swing of his arm, and the portrait was back in place.

Amity opened the shutters and followed the two back to the light and warmth of the sitting room. The Colonel receipted the bill with a quill pen, then brought out a stout wallet and put five ten-dollar bills into Aunt Keziah's hand.

Bessie served glasses of cider and slices of pound cake. Sipping the amber liquid, Amity wondered if she dared ask about Sam.

"How are the children?" asked Aunt Keziah. "I haven't seen them for a long time."

"Loammi began the practice of law in Cambridge this month, and Clarissa's been visiting Sally in Boston. She likes it so well I think she may attend Mrs. Snow's school one day."

"And what of George?"

"He's been ill of a sore throat since I got home, else I'd have brought him over to meet your young nephew. He's seven now, and can't find time for half the things he wants to do. It's a mercy that school takes up most of his day, else I'd be worn out."

"Is the school nearby?" asked Amity.

"A mile down the road," said the colonel. "It's nothing

fancy, but the children get a good solid foundation there. If your brother is old enough, it might be well to enter him."

School. That was the answer to Tim's loneliness. There he'd meet other boys his age; he'd have someone to play with.

"Would Monday be a good day for him to start?" she asked.

Aunt Keziah cleared her throat. "Let's not be hasty."

"Oh, come now, Keziah. Monday's not a day too soon," the Colonel said firmly. "The boy should rightly go."

"He should," agreed Amity.

Aunt Keziah frowned. "Why can't you leave well enough alone? Darius can teach him. There's no telling what this may lead to."

"Just some learning, I hope," said Amity. How wrong she was, she was not to know until later.

14

The Secret of the Vine-covered Door

When Amity set out with Tim on Monday morning, she realized that this was the first time either of them had ventured away from Aunt Keziah's home since their arrival in Newbridge. On their walks they had not stepped off her land except to stroll along the canal. Neither Bessie nor Aunt Keziah had left the house during that time. Colonel Baldwin's hired man fetched staples from the village and delivered their few messages. Why the two women never went into the village, Amity did not know. Were they simply content with the pleasures of home life? Or was there some reason why they did not wish to go to the village?

The crisp air held a hint of frost. Only the oak leaves clung to the trees, their red-browns glowing. A chipmunk darted across the road and perched in a crevice of a stone wall, its tiny chest palpitating as it gave a shrill cry.

"I wish I had brought Ebeneezer," said Tim.

"Mice don't belong in school," said Amity firmly.

As they passed the Baldwin house Tim looked about

for the youngest son of whom the Colonel had spoken. But there was no sign of George, and they continued on into the village without seeing any child of school age. When they came to the square building just off the village green, they understood why. School was already in session. From open windows came the sound of youthful voices singing a hymn.

Tim hung back, dragging on Amity's hand. "I'm afraid. I don't want to go in."

"You mustn't grow up to be a dunce," she remonstrated.

The heavy wooden door squeaked as it opened. Some forty children of various ages stopped singing and swiveled their heads around to see who might be arriving so late. At the front of the room a slight young man in a black coat laid down the ruler he'd been using as a baton.

"Is this a new pupil?" he asked. He had a serious mien.

"Yes, I'm sorry he's beginning late, but we have been in Newbridge only a short time," explained Amity.

"I thought you must be new here," said the teacher. His cheeks had reddened and he appeared flustered. "He has missed a few weeks' work, but perhaps he can catch up." He paused, then added, "My name is Guy Pitts."

"My brother's name is Timothy Lyte. Is there anything you need me for, or should I go now?"

The children had begun to laugh and chatter, and Amity had to raise her voice. Mr. Pitts tapped the desk with the ruler.

"Pupils," he said, "please to be quiet."

There was a titter, then an uneasy silence.

"Thank you, Miss Lyte. I'm sure Timothy can answer any questions." Mr. Pitts bowed, and Amity shut the creaking door behind her, glad to be out of range of those eighty gimlet eyes.

Now that she was in the village, she might as well look about. They had hurried through so quickly the first day that she had hardly seen a thing. A window gay with bolts of calico and damask caught her eye. A sign above the door read Jedediah Rapp, Proprietor. A fussy little old man with a round face and steel-rimmed spectacles bustled forward when she entered.

"I've just got a new shipment of laces and ribbons from France," he said, rubbing his hands together. "Care to see them?"

Ribbons? They were just what she needed to go with her new frocks. While she fingered lavender and green satin lengths, the shopkeeper ventured, "Both of those would look good with your hair. Why don't you buy the two?" His smile was ingratiating.

"I haven't any money with me," she explained. "I came out for another reason, and thought I'd see what you had."

"If you want to take the ribbons with you, I could put the amount down in my book. That's what I do with lots of the ladies."

Aunt Keziah had been so generous, surely she would not mind if Amity bought a ribbon or two. "Very well," she said, "set them down to the account of Mrs. Keziah Woods."

The eagerness vanished. "Her that was a Lyte?" asked the man. Was she imagining his coolness?

"That's right," she said. "My name is Lyte, too. I'm Darius Lyte's daughter."

"Humph! One of them Lytes. Sorry, Miss, you can't

have that ribbon. Jedediah Rapp don't do business with Tories." He began winding the ribbons on their spools with angry haste.

She couldn't have been more surprised if he had struck her across the face. "Tories!" she stormed. "We're not Tories! Besides, that war was fought thirty years ago!"

"I ought to know, I was in it," spat the man, "and I'll have naught to do with them that turned traitor."

Amity marched out of the store, her heels rapping sharply on the floor. She wished the stuffy little man were stretched out on the planks and she could stamp out some of her indignation on him. She slammed the door behind her, and glared at a plump housewife on the steps. Was she another villager who hated the Lytes?

She was still angry as she stalked homeward. Neither the sun's warmth nor the birds' singing soothed her. The injustice of the man's rebuff rankled. So did her resentment toward Aunt Keziah and Bessie. Why had they let her step unprepared into such a situation? Why hadn't they given her one word of warning?

Trembling, she left the road and walked up the avenue of rowan trees. The vine-covered doorway seemed to mock her. There's a reason why I'm never opened, it seemed to say. Everybody knows about it but you, Miss Amity Lyte. Everyone but you.

She clenched her fists and rounded the corner to the older part of the house. The courtyard was the picture of peace. Bees droned among late blossoms. The pungent fragrance of pepper relish drifted out the windows to mingle with the musky scent of chrysanthemums. Aunt Keziah and Bessie were stripping the pods from shell beans while Darius was deep in a book.

Aunt Keziah looked up. "Did you have any trouble finding the school?" she asked.

"Not finding the school," exploded Amity. "But I had plenty of trouble at a draper's shop!" She sat down on a bench and burst into tears, covering her face with her hands. "Oh, Aunt Keziah, why didn't you tell me that people hate us?" She sobbed. "Why didn't somebody tell me?"

Her voice harsh with emotion, Aunt Keziah said, "Darius, in heaven's name tell your daughter what she has every right to know."

"I was only trying to shield her," her father said.

"Shield her! You've done her more harm by keeping the truth from her!"

Amity looked up to see Aunt Keziah glaring at her father. He lifted a shaking hand to brush drops of perspiration from his forehead and cleared his throat nervously.

"Well," he began slowly, "you must know that my parents died when I was young, and I lived here with Aunt Keziah and my grandparents. When I was growing up, there were two men I came near to worshiping. They both had brilliant minds and were kind enough to take an interest in me. One was Loammi Baldwin and the other was Benjamin Thompson, now Count Rumford. They used to let me look at the apparatus they built, and watch some of their experiments. They had attended Professor Winthrop's lectures at Harvard, and had many advanced ideas about the sciences. Loammi was thirteen years older than I, and Ben four years older.

"Before the war broke out, feeling ran high in Woburn, just as it did throughout all the colonies. But after Lexington and Bunker Hill, there was downright hatred of the British and everybody who was on their side. Loammi Baldwin gathered men together and went to Cambridge to serve under General Washington. Ben Thompson had gone to New Hampshire, married a wealthy widow, and had a child, Sally. People there doubted his patriotism, and he came back to Woburn to his mother's house. He said he was looking for a commission in the Continental Army."

"And what about you, Father?" asked Amity.

"For some time I couldn't make up my mind. All my life I'd been taught to respect law and order, and some part of me agreed with British rule. But I could see injustice in it, and I came to feel that the colonies had a more worthy cause. Yet I could not bring myself to bear arms with the purpose of taking human life. I hoped to find a way to serve the colonies that seemed right to me.

"One day Loammi came home from Cambridge and invited me to join his regiment. I said I'd never make a soldier, though I'd like to help somehow. That same day Ben Thompson came secretly to our house and asked me—" His voice faltered. He put one hand over his eyes and stopped.

"Go on," said Keziah. "She might as well know it all."

"He asked if I would work with him collecting information about the patriot forces. He had a way of sending messages to the British in Boston by writing with invisible ink between the lines of a harmless message. His accomplice in Boston knew the chemical that would bring out the secret writing. He suggested that if I joined Loammi's company I'd be in a better position to find out things that were significant." His eyes were hot with the memory. "He asked me to inform on his closest friend and mine!"

How could anyone be so monstrous? Amity shook with indignation. "What did you do, Father?"

"I went to Loammi and told him of Ben's proposition. But I might as well have been talking to a stone wall. He refused to listen. He claimed Ben Thompson was his friend, and he would not believe Ben would betray him or his country unless he had incontrovertible proof. And of course I had none."

Keziah sighed. "Loammi would never listen to bad reports. He has always refused to see evil in anyone."

Amity couldn't imagine a more tortuous position. "What did you do then?"

"What could I do? I was sure I'd lost Loammi's friendship, and I wanted none of Ben's. That very night Jedediah Rapp brought a mob of half-drunk patriots out here with a barrel of tar and a feather tick. They were roaring that they'd break the house down if I didn't come out. Loammi must have told someone that I wouldn't join up."

"Surely Colonel Baldwin wouldn't send a mob!" protested Amity.

"He may not have sent them, but who else could have told them of my refusal to fight?" Darius asked bitterly. "At any rate, they said they had a little persuasion to make Tories change their sentiments. They threw rotten eggs and turfs at the house. My grandmother was ill. My grandfather pushed me out the back door, and went to the front to quiet them. I should never have let him, but I was young and used to obeying him." Darius put his head in his hand again.

Amity could almost see her great-grandfather at the front doorway, his white hair like a nimbus in the torchlight. "Did he quiet the mob?" she demanded.

"Not the way he intended," said Aunt Keziah. "He had spoken only a few words to them when he was taken with a seizure and fell across the threshold. When I got to him, he was dead."

"Oh, Aunt Keziah!" Amity was horrified. She could see her aunt, young and anguished, stooping over her father, tugging his body inside, while the mob drifted away, leaving the barrel of tar to harden in the yard and the feathers to blow about on the wind. And she imagined Aunt Keziah closing the great door in a frenzy, turning the key with tragic finality. No wonder the door had not been opened since. She could understand it all now, all but one point.

"What about Sally Thompson?" she asked. "How dare she come to Woburn, the daughter of a traitor?"

"Ben deserted her mother when Sally was a baby, and folks feel sorry for her," said Bessie. "Ben went off after another mob came to get him, though that time Colonel Baldwin was home and calmed them down with victuals and his best Madeira. Ben went to England, got a commission, and fought on the British side in New York. There are folks on Long Island who hate him still for tearing down their church, baking bread on the grave stones, and cutting down all the apple trees for firewood though there were plenty of other trees. Later he went back to Europe and picked up honors and titles as if they were windfalls."

"But you cook on one of his stoves." Amity tried not to sound accusing.

"Loammi arranged for that," said Aunt Keziah. "And it is a big help to Bessie. Ben's a brilliant fellow despite his faults, and that stove is only one tiny part of his accomplishments. In Bavaria he reorganized the army and improved the country's economy so successfully he was given the title of Count Rumford."

"Did Sally and her mother ever see him again?"

"His wife never did. Poor soul, she died when Sally was eighteen. Four years later Ben sent for Sally and she spent three years with him in England and in Bavaria where she was given the title of Countess. She's been back in this country for six years now, and Loammi says that she is far happier here than she was with her father."

Amity sat quietly, sorting out her thoughts. One returned to plague her.

"Why do people here still think Father was a Tory?"

"They took my running off as proof of my guilt. And since I never enlisted in the Continental Army, they were sure of it, though all I did was to refrain from fighting. I went to New York and met your mother, and you know the rest."

Only too well she knew how death and disaster had finished the second chapter in her father's life. She closed her eyes in painful memory. But when she opened them and saw the sunlit garden where asters bloomed and birds sang she realized that life was not all shadows and sorrow. Surely there must be some way Father could be cleared of a false reputation, and walk freely among the people of his own town.

15

"His father's a Tory!"

That afternoon Amity set out to meet Tim, her mind in a turmoil over her father's disclosures. Just beyond the Baldwin mansion she saw a number of children, and heard their voices. Tim must be among them. How good that he had already found friends! As she drew near, however, she realized that the words were not a song, but a cruel verse chanted over and over by a taunting circle at the frightened boy in its center.

> "Timothy Lyte is scared to fight!
> His father's a Tory, and he's not sorry."

Amity broke into a run. "How dare you torment my brother?" she stormed. "You ought to be ashamed, teasing a little boy."

To her surprise Tim said thickly, "I am not little, Amity." His lip was swollen, and there was blood on his chin. "But I don't know what a Tory is."

"Hah!" A derisive jeer swept the group. A boy called out, "A Tory's a traitor, that's what, and we don't want any around here. Your father was a Tory. And my father says there's no room in Newbridge for Tories. Yaaaah!" He put his thumbs in his ears and waggled his fingers at Timothy.

For the second time that day Amity could hardly speak for choking anger. When she found her voice she came close to screaming. "Stop it! Our father was *not* a Tory!"

The children stuck out their tongues and chorused, "Nyahh!" She might as well have saved her breath. Seizing Tim's hand, she hurried him along the road. She couldn't get away from those ignorant little bumpkins fast enough. She was so upset that she hardly saw the two men alighting from a chaise at the path leading to Aunt Keziah's house. Only when they started to walk under the arched rowan trees did she recognize them. One was Luke Fenwick. The other was Mr. Strobo Dix, his companion on the *George Washington*. What were they doing here? For a moment she forgot her fury at the children.

Luke Fenwick bowed when he saw her, surprise and pleasure showing on his smooth face. "I've been wondering when I'd meet you again," he said. "And how is your little brother? Been climbing up on top of any packet boats lately?"

Tim glared, kicking at the pebbles in the path. Mr. Dix spoke for the first time. "You wouldn't happen to know who owns this estate?" he asked.

"It belongs to my aunt, Mrs. Woods," said Amity proudly.

"It doesn't look as if anybody lived in it," said Mr. Dix, the corners of his mouth turning down.

"This is just the addition," said Amity. "My aunt lives in the older part."

"I'd be grateful for an opportunity to talk with her."

Amity could think of no way to refuse his request. As she led them around toward the ell, Mr. Dix studied the house.

"Three full stories and four chimneys," he said. "There must be four corner rooms on each floor, all with fireplaces."

Amity scarcely heard him, for Luke had slipped his hand under her elbow. "You little minx, you pulled the wool over my eyes with your talk of a cottage."

She jerked away angrily. She had honestly expected to find Aunt Keziah in a cottage. But Luke was saying, "I wonder if I might be permitted to take you for a drive some time?"

If he weren't quite so forward I might like to go driving with him, thought Amity. She'd seen scarcely anything of the district. And she had begun to wonder if she would ever hear a friendly word again.

"Perhaps," she answered, caution delaying her decision. Then they were in the courtyard, and she was introducing the callers to her aunt and father. When they were all seated, Strobo Dix looked at Aunt Keziah from under his eyelids.

"I am looking for a piece of property on the canal," he said. "Your home appears too spacious for you, and I wonder if you would care to dispose of it. Of course it is run down and in need of repairs."

"Run down?" asked Aunt Keziah. "Indeed!"

"All that old molding and carving should come off.

And the trees should be cut down, and of course the vines. But I'm prepared to make you a fair offer despite that."

"Offer?" said Aunt Keziah. "You mean you want to buy it? Why?" A vein in her neck began to throb.

"I need a large place," said he, "with lots of bed-chambers."

"This house is not for sale!" snapped Aunt Keziah.

If Mr. Dix was disappointed, he did not show it. He pulled a card from his pocket and laid it on the table. "Very well, madame, I shall look elsewhere," he said, "but here is my address in case you should change your mind."

"I won't," said Aunt Keziah shortly. She rose, indicating with an imperious glance that the interview was over.

Mr. Dix got to his feet and started off, Luke Fenwick at his heels. As he passed Amity, the young man said in a low voice, "I'll be back again to see you now that I know where you live."

Why hadn't he come straight out and asked in front of her father for permission to call? That was what any proper young man would do.

Before she could reply he had passed by, and Amity gazed at his retreating back in vexation.

Aunt Keziah had resumed her seat and her fingers were drumming on the arms of her chair. Two bright pink spots glowed on her cheeks. "I don't trust that Mr. Dix," she said, "or the young man with him. How did you come to meet them, Amity?"

"On the packet, coming from Boston," said Amity. She told how Luke had rescued Tim as the vessel slid under the bridge.

"Perhaps I was overhasty in my judgment," said Aunt

Keziah. She looked at Tim standing beside her, and gave him a fond smile. Instantly her face sobered. She took his cheeks between her palms and said, "Oho! What has happened to our boy?" She examined his bruised lip and blood-stained chin.

"The boys were yelling at me on the way home from school, and when I tried to get away, one of them hit me." Tim sniffed and drew the back of his hand across his nose.

"What were they saying?" queried Aunt Keziah.

In close mimicry of the taunts, Tim chanted,

> "Timothy Lyte is scared to fight!
> His father's a Tory, and he's not sorry!"

Aunt Keziah stood up, her eyes flashing. "Will there be no end to it? They haven't forgotten yet and they're even teaching their children such beastliness!" she cried. Then one side of her face seemed to slip, she gave a hoarse moan, and collapsed. Her body fell inertly against the chair, and lay in a crumpled heap on the stones of the courtyard.

16

Not Worth a Continental

Amity, Darius, and Bessie carried the unconscious woman to her bed. Her breathing was almost imperceptible. Gently the young woman and the old removed her stiff bodice and voluminous skirt, and unlaced her stays. They wrapped a soft dressing gown about her chilled body and covered her with blankets, setting a stone jar filled with hot water at her feet.

"We must have a physician," said Amity. With shaking fingers she scrawled a note to Colonel Baldwin, and gave it to Tim. "Run like the wind!" she said. "The Colonel will send someone to fetch the doctor."

Within an hour Dr. Derby arrived, his stock awry, his wispy hair blown from the drive. Amity watched as he examined Aunt Keziah. While he was feeling her pulse, Aunt Keziah's eyelids fluttered, and she moaned. Minutes later she opened one eye and looked at the doctor in anguish. "You'll be all right," he said cheerfully. "It's high time you had a rest."

In the sitting room he told Amity, "She may regain the

use of her right side, or she may not. The important thing is that she be kept free from anxiety. She's had too much of that in her lifetime."

In the days that followed Bessie and Amity took turns keeping watch at the bedside. Night after night Bessie went without sleep, apparently unwearied by her vigil. "This is nothing to what Miss Keziah did for her mother," she protested when Amity urged her to rest, "and for her husband, too, poor young man."

"Was Aunt Keziah married long?" It was difficult to imagine her with a husband.

"Three years at the most. They lived here 'cause the old folks thought Miss Keziah was too frail to go away. But her, she was the mainstay of the family. A pillar of strength, she was." Bessie wiped away a tear that wandered down her plump cheek.

"Did she have any friends to help her?" asked Amity.

"Some came, but she wouldn't see them. The night her father died and she locked the door, she said she was locking out the world. And she kept her word. You notice how she dresses in the old style still. And not even a newspaper comes to this house to remind her of what's going on outside."

"Doesn't she know anything that's happened? That General Washington is dead, and Mr. Jefferson is President?"

"She only hears what Colonel Baldwin tells her, nothing more."

"How did she know about Tim and me?"

"The Colonel found out. He has ways of knowing things," said Bessie mysteriously.

"Why did she let Colonel Baldwin come to see her when she was determined to keep entirely to herself?"

"Because he wouldn't take no for an answer. And she finally realized she couldn't do everything alone."

Slowly Aunt Keziah began to recover from the shock. She could see with one eye. She could lift one feeble hand and point at things she wanted. And she attempted to mouth words. Amity dreaded her desperate efforts to communicate, when her purple lips grimaced and hoarse, unintelligible sounds emerged.

One evening Colonel Baldwin came. Amity led him into Aunt Keziah's room, and knew she had acted wisely, for one side of her aunt's mouth curved in a smile, and her eyes held a faint pleasure. She pointed at the drawer in her bedside table, and made one of the noises that so distressed Amity.

"She wants you to take something out of the drawer," said the Colonel. "Open it and see what's there."

There were two brass keys. Amity took them out and Aunt Keziah painfully gestured toward the sitting room and the door beyond.

"I think she wants you to be her business agent," said Colonel Baldwin heartily. "Is that right, Keziah?"

One eyelid drooped in affirmation.

"Come along then, Mistress Amity."

The paneled hallway with its carved moldings was quiet with a locked-in hush. In the parlor Colonel Baldwin closed the shutters, then held the candle while Amity turned the key in the little door behind the portrait. He lifted the heavy box down and stood aside while she unlocked it.

Lifting the lid, she peered curiously at the contents.

She took the topmost yellowed note and held it near the candle. *United States, Fifty Dollars* was printed on it. *This bill entitles the bearer to receive fifty Spanish milled dollars or the value thereof in gold or silver, according to a Resolution of Congress published at Philadelphia, November 2, 1776.*

A Continental bill! She'd heard about them all her life. They had depreciated in value until they were worth at most a penny for each dollar, and the phrase "Not worth a Continental" was a byword for utter lack of value.

Scarcely able to believe her eyes, she examined the bill again. "This money is worthless," she said.

"Not to your aunt," said the Colonel. "She gave her money to the Continental cause in good faith, and she believes these bills are as valuable as when she bought them."

Amity looked at him in astonishment. "Have you been giving her full value for these notes since 1776—twenty-nine years ago? She could not believe it. Yet it was possible. Aunt Keziah had cut herself off from the world since that time, and would not know of the notes' devaluation.

Mr. Baldwin gave her an earnest glance. "Could I tell her that the government in which she had invested all her funds had failed to support its legal tender, especially when I was a member of the committee to sign the paper money? She would have been forced to sell her home when real estate values were at rock bottom. Where could she and her aged mother have gone? To the almshouse? I had no choice then, and I have none now, but to make good my country's debt. There are other losses for which she can never be recompensed."

"You mean that Aunt Keziah has been living on your charity all these years?" she asked, her voice trembling. "And that all of us are dependent upon your generosity now?" She should be grateful. Why did pride prick her to this outburst?

"There's no charity involved," said Colonel Baldwin brusquely. "It's a matter of honor, my country's and my own. Now hand me the fifty dollars, and I'll receipt your statement and give the remainder to Keziah. Hurry, we must not keep her waiting."

Reluctantly Amity put the bill into his hand. She would accept the Colonel's help this time. But she would try her utmost to find some way to make the Lyte family independent before the Colonel came again. Whether to tell her father posed a weighty problem. Would the knowledge spur him to some effort? To teach calligraphy? Or painting? a small voice whispered in the back of her mind. But where could he find a post? Probably not one person in Woburn would hire him as a teacher. Moreover, the knowledge of his aunt's debt to Colonel Baldwin might widen the rift between the two men.

She squared her shoulders. If anyone were to find a solution, it would have to be herself, though how a girl of sixteen might support a family of five she could not imagine. Then she recalled Bessie's words—"A pillar of strength." Aunt Keziah had been that for years to her family. Perhaps her niece could, as well.

17

A Second Offer

One bright afternoon Amity raked leaves at the front of
the house, glad to be released from her bedside vigil.
How invigorating the air, and how welcome the sunlight!

A long blast from a horn sounded and she leaned on
her rake to watch a barge, piled high with hogsheads
and kegs, float into view and ponderously pass by and
out of sight. The canal's continuing parade of crafts was
a never-ending source of delight. A packet boat proceeding smoothly along the narrow ribbon of water between
field and meadow and woodland still seemed something
of a miracle. To think that ten years ago the canal had
been little more than a dream in men's minds. And now
it was carrying goods and people from far points on the
Merrimack in New Hampshire all the way to Charlestown. No wonder Sam was proud of his part in the
achievement.

It was a long time since she had seen Sam. If only she
might talk things over with him, she might be able to
solve her problem. She had seized upon a score of ideas,
from a post as French teacher to working again as a

spinner, and rejected each one because in her heart she knew she was needed at home. A dozen times a day Bessie asked what to cook or clean. Tim's need for her was evident. Each afternoon when he came back to the house he would shout, "Amity, I'm home!" and she would drop whatever she was doing to hurry to meet him. He seemed to be happier at school, and she assumed he was now on friendly terms with the other pupils. Aunt Keziah was so frail, her hold on life so tenuous, that Amity was afraid to leave her for more than short periods. No, however she earned money, it must be within these four walls.

One day she had gone through the front of the house listing furniture and bric-a-brac. But could she sell them? No one in Woburn would give her what they were worth, and she could not ask Colonel Baldwin's help. But there must be an answer somewhere!

She took a fresh hold on the rake and swung it vigorously under the rowan trees, admiring the scarlet berries. Robins and jays darted among the branches, feasting on the clusters. Beneath a shrub, green eyes looked at the birds. The white and orange cat crouched there, the tip of its tail waving. If Aunt Keziah could see it!

Brandishing the rake, Amity advanced on the cat. She called out a threatening "Sssscccc!" When the animal ran down the road she had a strange satisfaction, as if Aunt Keziah had said "Well done."

The path was thick with leaves. She cleared it and paused before the broad front door. The covering vines had turned deep purple and magenta. Handsome they might be, but they did not belong there. Her fingers itched to tear them away, to free the doorway from its barrier. She mounted the wide steps and was stretching out her hand when a voice turned her swiftly around.

"I said I'd come back to see you. Would you like to go for a drive today?" Luke Fenwick stood looking up at her, the sun glinting on the buttons of his blue coat. He took off his hat and held it against his chest.

"I couldn't," she said, going down the steps slowly. "My aunt was taken seriously ill after you left that day, and I wouldn't think of leaving her."

"Is she very ill?" He sounded more curious than solicitous.

"I fear so." Tears filled her eyes.

"She may die." His words were more statement than question.

Amity nodded. Suddenly the future looked bleak and frightening. She dreaded a world without Aunt Keziah.

"Then you'll come into ownership of the house. Unless your brother was lying that day."

Something in his tone made her angry. "Of course he was not lying," she said coldly.

"I should think you'd be glad to sell this old ark. It's no place for a young pretty girl like you." His smile was ingratiating.

"An old ark—this?" She looked up at the stately facade. "No thank you. I'd have no wish to sell, even if I could. It's not mine yet, you know." She picked up the rake and jerked its teeth through a drift of yellowed leaves.

He kicked at a fallen twig. "I've had the devil's own time trying to find a place to suit Mr. Dix. He wanted something in this area, and no one will sell."

Did he expect her to give up her family's home just to satisfy Mr. Dix? "Why doesn't he build a place for himself?"

"He's thinking of it. But he's had trouble finding land. Some folks have exaggerated ideas about the value of their holdings on the canal. The only place we could get is beside that swamp." Luke pointed to a low area about a quarter of a mile down the canal in the direction of Woburn Village.

"I can't imagine why anyone would want to build a house on a marsh," said Amity.

"It was that or nothing," Luke said. He put his hat on his head, tapped his fingers against the top of the crown, and added, "Perhaps next time you'll have a different answer."

"Never!" she cried. But inwardly she was wondering. Would the time come when the house would have to be sold? Days had passed since she had learned the truth about the money in the Bible box. And in that time she had not come up with one feasible plan.

When Luke was out of sight, she looked up at the vine again. Should she tear it down? Then she thought of Aunt Keziah. It would be a pity to upset her. Better to leave the vine as it was.

It was time she went in, for Aunt Keziah might be needing her. She had washed her hands and smoothed her hair when a knock sounded on the door. She opened it to see Guy Pitts, the schoolmaster.

"I've come to inquire about Timothy," he explained. "I wonder why he has not come to school since that first day."

She gestured him into the sitting room. "But Tim has been going to school every day," she protested. "He leaves here with a lunch each morning, and comes home at the regular time in the afternoon."

"That's easy enough. He has only to watch out for the other children and return when they do. I dare say he's been playing in the woods all day."

Amity could hardly believe her ears. "I can't understand why he would do that," she said. She would wait until Mr. Pitts left, then get the truth out of Tim.

Bessie bustled in with gingersnaps and milk. Guy Pitts munched appreciatively on a cookie. "I wonder what happened to discourage Tim that first day," he said.

The first day. Amity saw again the ring of jeering children and heard their taunts. Almost without thinking she repeated the verses they had chanted.

Guy Pitts listened quietly. "I was afraid of something like that from what I overheard in the schoolyard. I shall speak to the pupils about it. Perhaps I could ask the parents to correct them too."

Amity's laugh was harsh. "Their parents!" she mocked. "They are the ones who have been feeding the children this hatred since they were babies!"

"I'm new in Woburn, but it's like my own home town in one way," said Guy. "People there find it hard to forget old wounds, too."

"My father never inflicted a wound on anyone!" said Amity sharply. "He thinks it's wrong to do injury to others—that's why he wouldn't fight—not because he was a Tory!"

"If the accusations are false, they should die down in time," said Guy.

In time. It was easy for him to say that, thought Amity. She wondered how he would feel if he had been in her place that morning at Jedediah Rapp's shop. Would he say thirty years was long enough?

18

Ghosts of Old Indian Fires

The next afternoon Sam Baldwin appeared. He submitted with admirable composure to Bessie's hug, and at her insistence went straightway to see Aunt Keziah, and patted her hand comfortingly. Clearly he was a welcome visitor in the household. Only when he spied Darius Lyte reading in a corner did Sam become uneasy.

"I'd like to ask your permission, sir, to take your son and daughter rowing on the canal," he said stiffly. Amity held her breath. She could almost hear her father's stern refusal.

While she waited, her heart pounding, Darius gave the young man a long level look. "Granted," he said, and returned to his book.

Sam flushed, but managed to say, "Thank you, sir." Giddy with surprise, Amity caught up her spencer, called to Tim, and the three set off for the Baldwin landing.

"This may be my last chance to take you boating before the canal freezes," said Sam. "Besides, Uncle said you've been cooped up in that house too much."

"It was kind of your uncle to think of me," said Amity, so demurely that Sam burst out laughing.

For all that the autumn was well spent, the weather was warm and mild. Filaments of gossamer clung to empty milkweed pods. Silver dusted the goldenrod, and the sumac lifted nuggets of faded blossom. It was hard to believe that the canal would soon be frozen over.

At the Baldwin estate the Colonel was supervising the storing of apples. Two ponies trotted about the orchard, a boy mounted on one and a girl on the other. Tethered to a post was a third pony.

The Colonel bowed. "Good day to you, Mistress Amity, and to you, too, Master Timothy. A fine day for boating."

Tim was speechless, looking at the boy and girl, the longing of a lifetime in his gaze.

"Clarissa and George," called the Colonel. "Come and meet a new neighbor." He waved his arm, and the children drew near on their mounts. "This is Timothy Lyte."

"Are those ponies your very own?" asked Tim shyly.

"Yes, mine is Star, and Clarissa's is Comet," said George.

"There's another pony here who needs a rider," said Colonel Baldwin. "Would you give him a little exercise?"

Tim gave the Colonel a worshiping look. Then Sam lifted the boy to the pony's back, adjusted the stirrups, and showed him how to hold the reins. He gave the steed a slap on its hindquarter, and it moved off, as steady as a rocking chair. Tim's face wore a huge smile.

"I seem to have lost a passenger," said Sam. But though he pulled down the corners of his mouth, he could not succeed in looking sad.

The boat was flat-bottomed with squared-off ends. Sam set some cushions and a basket of apples aboard, helped

Amity in, and settled himself at the oars. The boat looked clumsy, but it seemed to skim over the quiet water.

They approached a raft of logs drawn by a team of lumbering oxen. Sam pointed to a water rat that swam alongside at what seemed to be twice the raft's speed.

"Those musquashes," said Sam. He struck the water with an oar and sent a shower of spray toward the swimmer. It submerged and disappeared under weeds. "They cause more damage than spring freshets."

"What can you do to stop them?" asked Amity.

"There's a bounty for them, but they'll never be wiped out. The only thing is to watch out for their holes and fill them in. Ho, there, look ahead, there's the bank watch now!" He waved an arm. "Hi, Ned!"

An old man with frizzled gray hair walked slowly along the towpath, carrying a large bag of straw over one shoulder and a staff in the opposite hand. He lifted the stick in salute. Sam nosed the boat toward the bank and pointed to a spot where the water swirled in a small eddy. "Found one for you, Ned."

"Fix it for me, Sam, like a good lad." The old man handed a fistful of straw to Sam, and held out his staff. Sam coiled up the straw, rolled up his sleeve, thrust his arm into the water, and poked the wad into the hole in the bank. Then he took the staff and tamped the straw in firmly.

"That should hold," he said, and tossed the staff at the man.

"It ought to. You had a good teacher," said Ned, catching the stick in his free hand. He pointed his thumb at himself so that Amity would have no doubt as to the teacher's identity. Then he gave her a wink. "Take care he don't lead you astray!"

Sam grinned and picked up the oars.

"What happens if there's a hole too large for him to fill?"

"He sends a messenger on a fast horse to the nearest repair station, and the wrecking crew comes in its boat. They whiz along with a pair of good horses, and they can forget about speed limits. I've seen them go close to six miles an hour. The boats carry clay, straw, stakes, rope, planks, and picks and shovels. When they get to the break the gang jumps out and starts working. If the bank is broken open, they drive down rows of stakes, wattle them with rope, and fill in the space with straw. That stops the water till they can drive in pile planking and fill up the breach with earth and stone."

"How do you know so much about it?"

"I've worked with them. When there's a break, everyone pitches in to help. What a husky lot that gang is, and tough! But they're good-hearted."

Minutes later they were gliding past a swamp, its rushes brown and sere. "When I was a little boy I was scared to death of that swamp," said Sam. "My cousins used to take me there and show me magic fire. They'd poke sticks down in the ground, then pull them up fast and hold a lighted torch over the hole as the stick came up. There'd be a pop and a blue light. They told me it was ghosts of old Indian fires."

"I've never heard of anything like that. What was it?"

"Just marsh gas," said Sam. "I know that now, but when I was younger they had me fooled. Especially when an old Indian called Joe Beaver used to come around. Has he been to your place yet?"

Amity shrugged. "I haven't seen one Indian since I've been here. Are there any?"

"In the summer a lot of them camp near the tavern at Horn Pond. They sell baskets and berries. Joe wanders around and sleeps in people's barns. He used to like your aunt's hayloft."

"I hope he's gotten over it," said Amity. She had no desire to have an old Indian poking around.

"Hey! Look over there!" Sam pointed to an area of filled land where stakes had been driven to mark a foundation. "Someone must be going to build. Whoever it is wants to have his place close enough to the canal."

"That must be where Mr. Dix is going to build."

"Dix—who's he? I don't know that name."

She blurted out the story, telling how Luke Fenwick had saved Tim's life and later appeared with Mr. Dix seeking to buy Aunt Keziah's house.

Sam listened quietly. "Don't feel overly grateful to Fenwick for helping Tim off the roof," he said. "That's just good sport for some boys, walking along the top one step faster than the boat's going. The worst they get is a bump or wetting."

"It looked dangerous to me," said Amity. "I think Mr. Fenwick was very brave."

"All right, he was brave," said Sam, as if he were telling her she could believe what she wished. He slapped at a gnat on his forehead. "I wonder why they wanted to buy your house. If a man's looking for a new home he usually comes alone, or brings his wife. Wouldn't you want to have a say in where you were going to live?" He gave Amity a sharp look.

"I suppose so," she said honestly. "But I should think any woman would love Aunt Keziah's house. It seems perfect to me."

"Then it shouldn't be sold," said Sam. "Why are you thinking about it?"

Should she tell him about the Bible box and its piles of Continental currency? It was his uncle who had been underwriting all their expenses. Would Sam think she was ungrateful to wish to be independent? She looked at the firm tilt of his chin, at his strong hands on the oars. If anyone could understand a desire for independence, it was Sam.

She poured out the whole tale. Suddenly she realized that she felt less troubled than she had in weeks. What a relief to share her burden! "What am I to do now?" she asked.

Sam pulled steadily at the oars. "There's an answer somewhere," he said. "When you're least expecting it, you may find it." They rode on in companionable silence. Then he gave a twist to the oars and propelled the boat to a landing. "Here we are at Warren's Tavern," he said. "Want to come with me while I pick up a newspaper for Uncle?"

She hesitated, remembering the draper at Newbridge.

"Nobody's going to say anything nasty to you," said Sam, "not while you're with me." He clenched his fists.

He made the boat fast and gave her a hand up. They watched a packet roll into sight, its colors gay as a rainbow. "We'd better get up to the tavern now unless we want to wait until all those people are taken care of. They're an overnight crowd, I'd say."

The inn's weathered walls had furnished hospitality for more than one generation of travelers, Amity decided. Just inside the door they entered a dusky room where a rotund man sat behind a circular bar in the corner. "Ho, there, Sam," he called out. "Here's a *Gazette* for your uncle." Tufts of white hair gave his pink face a cherubic look. "Bless me if there aren't more guests coming than I can take care of. If I were younger I'd build on a new wing. There are travelers enough to fill a dozen taverns nowadays."

Amity walked down the hill beside Sam, watching the people climbing to the inn. There were groups of mothers and fathers and children. One family caught her eye. Three laughing boys and a girl tagged after their parents. Her throat ached. Why couldn't she be that girl? Why had her happiness ended so abruptly?

At the boat Sam handed her the *Gazette*. "Want to look at the news?" he offered.

It was a long time since she had seen a paper. She opened it and started to read, but couldn't concentrate. An idea was fluttering just out of reach. Suddenly her mind fastened upon it with such clarity that she cried out, "I've found the answer! I know it will work!"

"It must be good," said Sam, "or you wouldn't look so happy."

"I'll turn the house into an inn," she said, her thoughts racing ahead. "One of the parlors will make an office and sitting room, and the other an extra dining room. The music room can double as a writing room for guests. There are eight bedrooms. That means we could take sixteen guests, or more, if we put up cots for children."

Sam gave the oars a flourish, waving them in the air so that drops spattered into the canal. "What a good idea!"

"The house won't have to be changed a bit," she went on. "Bessie can get the meals—you know how she loves to cook. Aunt Keziah needn't know a thing about it. And Father—" All at once the dream faded.

What about Father? She would have to tell him her plan. And she would have to give him a valid reason for opening the house as an inn. Like Aunt Keziah and Bessie, he believed there were funds enough to carry them along indefinitely.

"How can I let Father know that your uncle has been providing for Aunt Keziah all these years?" she asked. "He feels hurt that Colonel Baldwin wouldn't believe him years ago." She sighed.

"If your idea is going to work, you've got to tell him sometime," said Sam practically.

"That's right," she admitted, grateful for his steady common sense.

"As for your father's feeling toward Uncle Loammi, no one can change that except your father. If he would only realize that Uncle is as generous in his judgments as with his apples! I've heard him say a hundred times that every man is entitled to his own opinion of what he thinks is right. That's why he has been so stanch in supporting Count Rumford. He hasn't forgotten they fought on opposite sides in the war. He says each individual had a right to choose for himself how he'd stand, but now that the war is over, we ought to work together. As he sees it, there's plenty of work to do."

Sam certainly admired his uncle. And Amity found herself agreeing with him. No one could be more kind and generous than Loammi Baldwin. If only Father would look clearly at the situation, he might change his attitude. Sam's last words echoed in her mind. Work to do. She had plenty of that ahead.

19

The Rowan Tree Inn

The next week the weather changed. A cold wind whistled down from the north, rattling the dried stalks of flowers and shaking a powder of snow on the ground.

To Amity's amazement, Tim agreed willingly to return to school. Questioned, he said that Colonel Baldwin had told him he might ride the pony any afternoon provided he attended school that day. The Colonel had also suggested that Tim walk to and from school with George and Clarissa. Amity let him go with a free mind, hopeful that in their company he might escape further persecution.

Alas for her hopes! One afternoon a bruised and disheveled Tim came hesitantly into the sitting room, George Baldwin at his heels. Tim drew the white mouse from his pocket and lifted it to his face, crooning, "You're not hurt, Ebeneezer?"

Amity ran to him, examined his purpling cheek, and said, "Have those children been tormenting you again?"

George burst out eagerly, "That Rapp boy said he was

going to feed Ebeneezer to his cat. You should have seen Tim hit him!"

A Lyte hitting anyone? Amity could scarcely believe it. But Tim looked at her defiantly, saying, "I couldn't let him get Ebeneezer. So I bashed him in the nose."

Amity bit back a rebuke. Fighting was wrong, Father said. But had Tim been wrong to strike out in defense of his pet? She watched the two boys twittering to the mouse as it crawled up Tim's arm and perched on his shoulder, looking about with its beady pink eyes. She couldn't help but be glad that Tim had saved the tiny creature.

Winter came in earnest. One storm after another brought drifts that covered field and pasture with white. Sleighs and pungs left icy ruts in the road. The canal was a smooth white strip.

Tim found an old sled in the barn. He and Amity spent many an hour coasting down a steep hill behind the house. And twice Colonel Baldwin took them for a drive with Clarissa and George in his shiny red sleigh. The bells on the harness jangled merrily, the horses' breath blew white in the frosty air, and the runners squeaked on the hard-packed snow.

Whenever she had a free hour, Amity slipped into the front part of the house. There was a tremendous task ahead. The draperies were faded and grimy, and had to be aired. The woodwork that had looked merely dusty needed to be washed. All the furniture had to be polished; some of the joints glued.

The rooms were so cold she tied an old shawl of Bessie's over her dress as she worked. She would do one room at a time, she decided, and started on a third-floor bedroom.

It was not simple to take cleaning equipment into the unused section of the house without being seen by Bessie or her father. Nor was lugging pails of hot water up two flights of stairs an easy task.

When at last one room was finished, she looked at the scrubbed and shining surfaces with triumph. She had made one chamber habitable, and there was no reason why she could not do others. But she longed to share her accomplishment.

Downstairs in the sitting room she found her father looking gloomily out the window. "It is not a good day for walking," he said restlessly, staring at bleak fields and black clouds.

Glowing with achievement, she said, "Would you like to take a walk to the third floor? I have something to show you."

Their footfalls echoed sharply on the bare stairs. On the top landing she threw open the door of the freshly cleaned chamber. "There! Doesn't it look inviting? If you were a traveler, wouldn't you like to sleep here?"

"What are you up to, Amity? Are you trying to tell me something?"

She nodded. "Aunt Keziah is not as well off as she believes. We'll have to find some way to live. Don't you think it a good idea to turn the house into an inn? That way we can stay here, all of us." She gave him a bright smile. Oh, let him be pleased, just this once, she prayed.

Darius sat down on the nearest chair and let his head fall forward in his hands. "If I were half a man," he said, "I'd be earning money and taking care of you all instead of—this."

"Don't blame yourself, Father." Amity stroked his dark

hair, so like Tim's except for the gray streaks. "I know you don't want to paint portraits ever again, and there's really no other work you can do, except teaching. And that's out of question here."

His shoulders shook. "I'm of no use to anyone. You'd be better off if I went away," he said in a muffled voice.

Better off without him! Amity felt anger and impatience bubbling up within her. In another second her rage boiled over. "Why don't you stop thinking about yourself?" she stormed. "Do you believe running away would do any good? There are a hundred ways you could be of use here. I certainly don't like doing all this work by myself. If you can't do anything else, you could at least help me get the house ready!"

She started to tremble, her words reverberating in her ears. Whatever had possessed her to speak so baldly to her father? He would never forgive her. Why, oh, why couldn't she curb her tongue? Half blinded with tears, she ran down the stairs.

She was struggling with the knob of the door into the sitting room when he came up behind her. "Daughter," he said in a shaking voice. "Daughter."

There was a tenderness in his tone she hadn't heard since before her mother's death. She turned and buried her face in his shoulder.

Two pairs of hands were surely better than one. Though Darius had never before washed woodwork or waxed a floor, he went at the tasks willingly, as if glad of purposeful activity. During the hours that he and Amity worked together, his habitual silence gradually gave way before her cheerful chatter.

Soon they found it necessary to include Bessie in the

secret. She was dumbfounded and distressed that her mistress's funds had dwindled. But when Darius asked if she would cook for the guests, she said she'd be honored.

Tim had to be told, too, the reason for their diligence. He looked forward to the prospect as a gay adventure. Only Aunt Keziah, lying in her bed, was told nothing.

If the house were to become an inn, it must have a name. For weeks Amity and Darius puzzled over a choice. In January, on one of his rare visits, Sam Baldwin suggested "The Lyte House"—at which they all chuckled. Amity thought of and discarded others—Middlesex Manse, the Canal Tavern, Newbridge Inn—but none seemed right. Then she recalled her first glimpse of the house as she looked up the pathway between the rowan trees. Why not name it after the trees?

The Rowan Tree Inn. The more she said it, the better she liked the name, and soon it sounded so natural she could not imagine the house being called anything else.

There should be a signboard set near the canal where travelers could see it and know that the big house with the arched trees was open for their custom. She envisioned a pale yellow panel with a rowan tree at one side, bright with clusters of crimson berries, and the name in dark green. She found a board in the shed and sketched in the outlines. Tim and George watched her admiringly, and George brought her three small pots of paint from the Baldwin's workshop. There was barn-red, yellow, and green.

She was struggling to lay the colors on when her father appeared. If only he would forget his determination never to paint again. Helplessly she put the brush aside. "It isn't coming out the way I intended," she said.

"It never does at first," he said. He peered at her work. "Not bad at all. You've quite a knack for it. But your colors are too crude. Try mixing a little yellow with the red for the berries. And put a touch of red into the green to tone it down."

"Could you show me how?" she begged, hoping he might pick up the brush and complete the sign.

He stretched out his hand toward the brush, then slowly withdrew it. "You're doing very well," he said. "Just keep on."

She could have wept for disappointment. But he had become so willing to help in other ways that she must not lose hope. That he had spoken words of encouragement was cause for gratitude.

She had another reason to be thankful. Aunt Keziah had improved to the point where she could sit up. She was regaining the use of her limbs, and what was more important to her—her tongue. She succeeded in saying words, with studied precision, to be sure, but she could make herself understood.

By March she was well enough to be helped from her bed to a wing chair. When Darius and Amity lifted the chair into the sitting room and placed it beside the fire, Aunt Keziah's smile was a reward in itself.

"I—had—forgotten—how—pleasant—this—room—is," she said, and waved her hand as if in benison at the plants, the slant-front desk, the table with its books and bowl of apples, and her embroidery frame. Each day she spent an hour or two there, contented. Amity busied herself with sewing. At Aunt Keziah's request she worked on the embroidery her aunt had begun before her illness. But she was impatient to go back into the front of the house to ready the rooms for occupancy. Some of her impatience must have shown in her jabs at the canvas as she sat before the frame one March afternoon, alone in the room with her aunt.

"Something—troubles—you?" asked Aunt Keziah.

A quick denial was on Amity's lips. Then she caught the faded blue eyes looking into hers, and she was ashamed of the months of deception. Aunt Keziah had a right to know what was going on. She had weathered worse difficulties alone. Like anyone else she hated being kept in the dark. How indignant she had been with Father when he had said he was trying to shield Amity. Surely illness had not sapped all of her courage.

"We're planning to use the new part of the house as an inn," she began. During her explanation Aunt Keziah's face expressed in turn incredulity, dismay, and finally acceptance. For long moments she remained silent. Then her face brightened, she pointed to the desk, and said, "Please—bring—me—the—key."

Amity opened the small door between the pigeonholes and withdrew a large brass key.

"The—door. Unlock—it!" commanded Aunt Keziah.

Trembling, Amity crossed the sitting room and went into the wide front hallway. She stood before the great front door, her hand shaking as she inserted the key in the lock. On this very spot her great-grandfather had died. Here where she stood Aunt Keziah had turned this very key to lock the door on a world she feared.

She hesitated, while the chill of the empty rooms

pierced through her gown, and the ghosts of the past swirled around her. She looked at the walls and floors she had worked so hard to freshen, and lifted her head. It was not right for this house to remain silent and unused. It had been built as a home, a place where people could love and laugh and find happiness. There might be fear and sorrow and death as well, but they were just as much a part of living. It was only right that new life might enter the house.

She put her hand on the key and gave it a strong twist. The unused lock resisted. She put more strength into the effort, and this time the metal parts moved and the key turned. She put both hands on the doorknob, and tugged at the broad door. The hinges squeaked, and the door swung inward, revealing the lacy network of vines that blocked the opening.

Amity tore at the fibrous curtain with both hands, wrenching the stems from the pilasters at either side.

Her heart beat like a triphammer as she looked out through the open doorway. Beyond the arch of bare rowan trees lay the canal, a long ribbon of ice winding through snow-covered fields. Above flared a brilliant sunset, its colors tinting the snow and ice in roseate hues.

Some would say it was a coincidence that the first time she looked out through this doorway she should see such a glory of color. But Amity felt differently. She would take it as a sign—a promise that the future would be as bright as the sky.

20

Beside the Towpath

One afternoon in late March Amity set out for the village with a letter to Mlle. Armand in care of Mr. Elijah Pratt of New Haven where she was serving as governess. Amity had written about her plans for the Rowan Tree Inn, and urged Mlle. Armand to come and visit when she was free.

The ice on the canal was porous and partly melted, and peppered with bits of leaves and bark. Yellow willow withes, tight red maple buds, and a few spears of green at the canal's edge hinted at spring.

As Amity walked along she saw that workmen were busy on Strobo Dix's land beside the canal. Where corner stakes had stood in the autumn, masons were now laying a foundation, their trowels moving swiftly from mortar to fieldstone.

This was no ordinary dwelling that Mr. Dix was erecting. Its front stretched a full sixty feet parallel with the canal. An ell stretched another sixty feet to the rear.

A tall young man broke away from a knot of workmen. "What do you think of the Dix House?" asked Luke Fenwick.

"It's large enough," Amity answered.

"It has to be, to accommodate all the travelers we hope to serve," he said, falling into step beside her.

"Travelers?" she asked, trying to hide her agitation. "Do you mean this will be an inn?"

"What else?" he asked. "You didn't think Dix was looking for a place to live, did you?"

He'd surely given that impression. But then, Luke had said at their first meeting that his partner wanted to invest in property along the canal. What better investment than an inn? Her heart sank. This place was a little nearer to Boston than her own. The packets would halt here first and travelers would be more apt to take rooms here than at the Rowan Tree Inn.

Luke was looking at her strangely. "Don't you like the idea of a tavern near your house? Are you afraid it will disturb your peace and quiet?"

She almost laughed in his face. But inwardly she was seething. Why hadn't Luke come right out and said what Strobo Dix was planning? If she had known, she might not have decided to turn Aunt Keziah's house into an inn, though what else she might have done she couldn't fathom. At least, she could be straightforward.

"Months ago I made plans to use my family's home as an inn," she said. "We have everything in readiness, and plan to open the first day the packets ply the canal this spring."

Luke's mouth fell open. "I'll be damned," he said. "I wouldn't have thought you had the mettle to start up an

inn—a girl like you that won't even go for a little drive."
He looked at her with a calculating eye. "You know you'll
probably fail. Why don't you sell out to us now, and save
yourself the grief of losing your last penny?"

He was probably right. She knew nothing about innkeeping, and she might have to sell the house eventually.
But she wasn't going to let Luke Fenwick see how
frightened she was.

"I won't sell," she said. She didn't trust herself to say
more.

Luke looked down at the ground and drew a circle
with the toe of his boot. He gave her a speculative
glance. "How about going into partnership? Strobo knows
this business backwards. Let me tell you how he plans
to save on the cost of building."

He pointed to the foundation. "You can see that this
has only a partial cellar. A full cellar costs too much;
besides the earth is too spongy here. A stone floor
would be expensive. Dirt with a plank or two laid over
it will be good enough. Upstairs no double floors, and
just single plank partitions. We won't waste time and
money building for eternity. How about letting us take
over your place to run? We could build on a cheap addition, and you'd get a share of the profit."

The effrontery of his suggestion! How could he have the
gall to suggest she would fail before she had even begun?
She felt the hot color burning in her cheeks. "What
makes you so sure I'm going to fail? Just because you're
a man doesn't mean you'll succeed and I won't. I wouldn't
let you take over my house if I were starving! Besides,
I have a secret you know nothing about that's bound to
make my inn succeed!"

She stamped away as he shouted, "Don't say I didn't give you a chance!"

Why had she made that statement about a secret? Bessie's good cooking was what she meant. Once travelers tasted her pies, her rolls, and succulent meats, they would never be satisfied with ordinary tavern fare. And if Luke and Mr. Dix were out to cut expenses, they'd probably serve barely palatable food.

She was still so furious after she had posted her letter that she decided not to return by the canal, but to cut across the fields rather than chance seeing Luke Fenwick again. As she walked over the meadows, her anger gradually cooled, and changed into firm determination. She could not allow herself to be discouraged by the threat of competition. The only course open was to go ahead as planned. Hopefully there would be travelers enough for both inns.

When Amity drew near home she saw Bessie just outside the barn door, a shawl thrown over her head and shoulders. With her was an unkempt, tall, thin old man in greasy, stained garments. His dusky face inscrutable, he fished inside a filthy jacket, drew forth a pipe and small leather pouch, and held them out to Bessie. She took them with disdainful fingertips.

"You can sleep in the barn tonight, Joe, and I'll give you some supper," she said, her tone not unkindly.

"Drink?" he asked.

"Water, or maybe milk," she said.

He spat out of the side of his mouth. "Joe go soon to Great Father. Joe need good drink."

"No," she said firmly, "you're not sick, so you don't need it."

He threw her a look of disgust and shambled into the barn.

"Who in the world is that?" asked Amity, drawing near.

"An old Indian called Joe Beaver. Miss Keziah used to let him sleep in the barn, but she always made him turn over his pipe and flint and steel to her so he wouldn't set the place on fire."

"What did he mean by a drink?"

"One time he was sick, so your aunt gave him some elderberry wine. He got lightheaded and cavorted around too much. He's been asking for it ever since. He's failed something terrible. You heard what he said about going to the Great Father. Indians have a way of knowing when their time is coming. I hope he don't die in our nice clean barn."

Bessie held the pipe between thumb and forefinger. It was of clay, with a figure incised upon the bowl. Curious, Amity bent for a closer look. In the clay was scratched the outline of a beaver, its broad head and flat tail unmistakable. Joe Beaver's trademark, she thought.

As soon as Bessie stepped into the kitchen she dropped the pipe and pouch on a shelf, poured water into a basin and scrubbed her hands. Another time Amity might have been amused. Now she could think of nothing but the new inn rising a scant half mile away. Would it mean the failure of the Rowan Tree Inn?

21

The First Guest

A week later the *George Washington* made its first trip through the canal. Amity was polishing an upstairs window when she heard the packet's horn tootling for the locks. She had forgotten during the winter how cheerily the horns punctuated the days. Waving her cleaning cloth, she ran downstairs.

"The packet—it's coming!" she caroled, hurrying into the kitchen.

Bessie looked up from her Rumford stove. "We've roast chicken and beef pie," she said, "and rolls ready to bake."

They waited until after the packet had coasted by, resplendent in fresh orange and blue and red paint. The driver wore a new red coat, and the horses had gilt rosettes on their harness in honor of the occasion.

But the packet did not halt in front of the Rowan Tree Inn as had been arranged in case passengers wished to get off. The gangplank was not shoved out to the bank, and not one traveler walked up the pathway, either at noontime or in the late afternoon.

"Some folks are missing a wonderful meal," said Amity that evening as they sat down to heaping plates.

Each day for a week Amity dusted in readiness for guests, and smoothed the freshly made beds. Bessie set pans of dough to rise and planned special meals. At noontime they waited in expectation. Again in the after- noon they watched the packet's deliberate approach, hoping it would stop beside the sign that swung so bravely at the canal's edge. But not one person ventured through the wide front door.

On the eighth day Amity was ready to give up. After days of tense anticipation her spirits had sunk to a low ebb. There was no point in preparing for guests who never appeared. The sun shone with surprising warmth. Would not today be a good time to give Aunt Keziah's room a thorough cleaning?

Amity slipped into her old frock. She got out buckets and cloths, and took the curtains down from the windows.

Bessie seemed affected with the same mood. After all, one could be keyed up for just so long. Today she would wash her hair.

Amity hung the freshly laundered curtains to dry in the yard, then scrubbed at the woodwork. At noontime she and Bessie carried Aunt Keziah out to the courtyard. Bessie brought out another chair for herself and spread her freshly shampooed hair across her shoulders.

The toot of the packet's horn sounded across the sunlit air. Amity went into the house for Aunt Keziah's feather bed and pillows, and tossed them over the line to fluff and air. She was back in the bedroom scrubbing at a stain in the floor when she heard her father's voice.

"Amity!"

For a moment she was alarmed. It was not Father's way to call out.

"Amity!" The call was nearer. "The packet has stopped."

She darted to the front window and was just in time to see a woman step daintily across the gangplank, lifting the skirt of her dove-gray traveling gown above the tips of her neat kid shoes. Her lavender parasol and reticule matched her small bonnet.

"Mademoiselle Armand!" Amity rushed forward, forgetful of her dripping hands, the torn apron tied over her worn gown, the locks of hair that straggled over her damp face. None of those mattered. The only thing she knew was that her dear teacher, her loyal, tender friend had arrived.

For the next hour all was confusion. Bessie's hair was dried and braided into its coronet. Amity managed to make herself presentable. Somehow lunch was prepared, and Aunt Keziah was brought into the sitting room. For the first time since her seizure she sat at the table with the others. And a festive occasion it was. Mlle. Armand exclaimed in admiration that Bessie must possess Gallic blood. How else could she excel all other cooks in this country?

After luncheon Aunt Keziah's head tipped wearily. Amity knew she must bring in the feather bed and pillows and make up the bed before the frail convalescent tired further. Bessie was already clearing the table.

Mlle. Armand's smile swept over them all. "And now if

I may be excused, I will go to my room. That is, if someone will help me with my luggage." In the confusion of her arrival, the bags had been set down in the hallway and forgotten.

Amity darted forward. But there was no mistaking Aunt Keziah's drained expression. For a moment she stood irresolutely.

"Perhaps Monsieur Lyte would be so kind as to assist." Mlle. Armand lifted her dark eyes to his.

He gave her a stiff bow. "With pleasure." He gestured her through the connecting door and followed with an eager step.

That evening Amity set the large table in the formal dining room, using silver and china she had found stored in the cupboards and mahogany sideboard. She brought in sprays of forsythia for the wall vases, and put nuts and mints in the crystal epergne. Their first guest deserved the best they could offer. Bessie, too, was inspired. Her roast mutton, riced potatoes, and creamed onions were perfection; her poundcake and ginger pears without compare.

"What an enchanting house you have!" exclaimed the Frenchwoman. "And what bountiful meals you provide. It is a pity that I am the only traveler to partake of your hospitality."

"I can't understand why no one else has stopped here," said Amity in bewilderment.

"Perhaps it is because they do not know your inn exists. Had I not recieved your letter I would not have come."

Darius Lyte threw her a quick look. "We can't write to every traveler," he said, "but we might post some notices in strategic places—say in the packets or at the terminus in Charlestown."

"And at the other end of the canal, at Middlesex Village," added Amity.

"An announcement in your handwriting would attract favorable attention, I am sure, Mr. Lyte." Mlle. Armand smoothed the cuff of her gown.

"Do you really think so?" Darius Lyte looked at her questioningly.

"I do indeed."

He went to the desk, picked up a pen, dipped it in ink, and began writing. Mlle. Armand cocked her head at Amity and gave her a quick smile. Was Amity imagining it, or did her expression hold a hint of conspiracy?

A few minutes later Darius Lyte turned about. "How does this sound?" he asked, and read aloud: "The Rowan Tree Inn, one mile north of Woburn Village, offers lodging and meals to travelers on the Middlesex Canal."

"*Très bien!*" Mlle. Armand clapped her hands in applause. Then she pursed her lips thoughtfully. "I wonder, though, does it do justice to your establishment? Might you not say how elegant and yet how comfortable are the rooms, and how superb the meals? And would it not be of import that your inn is situated about midway along the canal, a half day's journey from either end?"

Darius clapped one hand to his forehead. "How do you think of these things?" he asked. "They never occurred to me."

"There is one thing more," said Mlle. Armand, rising. "If there were a sketch of this house, the merest suggestion of its beauty, travelers might be attracted to that as well." She gave him a bright look. "I am sure that would not be difficult for a man of your ability." Then she stepped up to Amity, touched her cheek against the girl's in a brief embrace, and said good night. A few minutes later Amity left the room. Her father did not even lift his head. He was bent over the desk, scratching away at a sheet of paper.

The next morning he had a notice completed.

The Rowan Tree Inn
Midway on the Middlesex Canal
One mile north of Woburn Village
Homelike Hospitality
Comfortable Rooms—Superb Meals

In the left hand corner he had sketched the front of the house with its arch of rowan trees. That day and the next he produced similar notices and arranged for them to be posted in the packets and in the terminuses.

A week later spring arrived in earnest. One afternoon two gentlemen and their wives came to the Rowan Tree Inn. They stayed only one night but were loud in their praise of its charm. From then on there was not a day when the Rowan Tree Inn was empty.

22

An Invitation

One evening, a week later, when the last traveler had gone upstairs, Amity sank down at the desk and picked up a pen with a hand trembling with fatigue. Mlle. Armand sat in a small rocker nearby.

Eight dinners at 50¢ each, wrote Amity. *Lodging for eight guests at 75¢ a night.* Now where were the figures for the supplies she had bought? She had put the paper somewhere. She fumbled among notes and lists. If only she were not so tired!

She had been on her feet since five o'clock, and running from one task to another, helping Bessie with the griddle cakes and sausages, setting bread to rise, carrying hot water upstairs, and waiting on tables. Tonight six rooms were occupied. That meant six rooms must be cleaned tomorrow, six beds changed, twelve sheets and pillow slips washed. And the tables in the dining room had yet to be laid for breakfast.

"*Chérie,* why do you not go to bed? It is past ten o'clock and you have not rested all the day." Mlle. Ar-

mand placed her soft fingers over Amity's roughened
hand.

It was all very well to talk about rest. But who could
sleep with so much yet to be done? "I cannot," she said,
"I've these accounts to do."

"Your father, I am sure, would take care of the matters
financial if you but asked. I would do it myself, but I
promised Mr. Pratt to return at the end of this week. I
am loath to go, leaving you so burdened. Is there no way
you can find domestics?"

Amity sighed. She had advertised locally for help, but
had received no replies. She was certain of the reasons.
The townspeople thought of her father as a Tory, and
none of them would work for him. "I'm afraid we'll
never find help in this town," she said.

"You might place an advertisement in the Boston
Gazette—like some of these." Mlle. Armand handed
Amity the paper.

Amity's eyes slid over notices of shipments of laces,
muslins, and nankeens. There were the Help Wanted
items. How eagerly she had scanned them less than a
year ago. Suddenly her eye lit upon a death notice.
*On the 14th ult. on board the Brig Mary from Martinique
for Boston, Monsieur René Leseigner, French gentleman,
aged 48, deeply lamented by all who knew him.* René
Leseigner—wasn't that Nicole's uncle, the one whose
arrival she so anxiously awaited? Amity read the notice
to Mlle. Armand, and told her about gay, impulsive
Nicole. "How sad for her! She has been looking forward
so long to his return!" Amity could sense the girl's grief.
"I will write and invite her to come and visit."

"Why not offer her work?" suggested Mlle. Armand.

Tired as she was, Amity wrote to Nicole that night. The day before Mlle. Armand was to leave, Nicole arrived. She brought greetings from Nance and Bill, and before the evening was over made them feel in close touch with the Trask family.

When Mlle. Armand departed, Amity clung to her. "I can't bear to have you go," she said.

"I may return later," said the Frenchwoman. "It depends upon certain matters." She set off toward the canal and the packet which was just coming into view. Amity would have followed, but a tardy guest appeared, requesting his bill so that he too might catch the boat. Amity's last glimpse of Mlle. Armand was of her slender back preceding Darius Lyte. He was carrying her luggage and seemed to hover over her with solicitude.

Nicole fitted tidily into the household. Were there carrots to prepare? She scraped and cut them into slivers. Were there rolls to make? She pinched pieces of dough, shaped them deftly, and tucked them into buttered pans. Amity wondered how they had ever managed without her.

One March afternoon Sam Baldwin came, carrying a bunch of branches with tight round buds. "I've brought you some apples," he told Amity.

"I don't see any apples," she protested. What was Sam up to now?

"They're right here," grinned Sam. "These are scions of the Baldwin apple tree brought to you by—"

"A scion of the famous Baldwin family," finished Amity, bursting into laughter.

He gave her a mock bow. "Come out in the orchard and watch me graft these onto your aunt's trees."

Glad to escape from her duties, she caught up a shawl. The spring air held a damp chill, but the sun was bright. Sam strode into the orchard. Before a sturdy tree he halted, and made a long diagonal cut across a branch. From his bundle he took a scion and cut its lower edge to match. Then he placed the two together, and bound them about with soft string.

"That branch will produce Baldwin apples, though the tree is a Jonathan." He moved from tree to tree, grafting new twigs onto the old stock.

Spring ripened into summer. Apple trees were transformed from gnarled skeletons to giant bouquets of fragrant pink and white. The scions Sam grafted bore blossoms and tender leaves.

From the canal-side site where Strobo Dix was building his tavern came daily the pounding of hammers and whine of saws. Amity could see its progress from her third floor windows—skeletal walls, a roof, and chimneys. Its bulk loomed like a menace. Would the Rowan Tree Inn survive the competition?

Sam made infrequent visits to Woburn. He would graduate from Harvard at the summer's end, and was studying and working with his cousin, Loammi Baldwin II. Though Loammi was practicing law, he hoped soon to visit England and the Continent to study methods of constructing bridges, roads, wharves, buildings, tunnels, and of course—canals. It was a wonderful age to be living in, said Sam, with all sorts of new ideas developing.

While she was with him, Amity was buoyed up by Sam's enthusiasm. But after he left, she was dragged down by the ceaseless work. The inn was becoming more and more of a burden to her, although her father now handled the accounts. She almost wished she had never thought of putting the house to such use. Then she would look at her father's lightened brow, at Tim, healthy and strong, and Aunt Keziah, recovered enough to walk alone, and she knew that the effort was worthwhile. Later, discouragement would nag, and she wondered if she would spend all her days catering to fussy, demanding travelers.

Then Bessie wrenched her knee. The doctor ordered her to rest for a week or ten days. Amity was stunned. Even as she urged Bessie not to worry, she was frantically searching for an answer to this new problem. Nicole echoed her dismay.

A few minutes later she asked, "What about Nance Trask?"

Amity gazed at her in astonishment. Nance, who hardly touched a broom? Nicole giggled. "I know what you are thinking," she said, "but Nance is strong, and she likes you, Amity. And she has changed. After you left she kept the house much neater. I think she may never have lived in a clean place before."

Two days later Nance arrived, bringing the twins with her. Soon she was sweeping and mopping. What matter that she splashed water and clattered buckets? She was cheerful, willing, and seemingly tireless. One day she confessed to Amity, "Seems like I couldn't see no point in trying to make my house look good till you showed me how. And this one's so elegant it makes a body want to do her best."

July passed. Bessie's knee improved, but Nance and the twins stayed on. Bill was due any day, as soon as he could find someone to take over Jezebel and the hackney

An Invitation / 181

coach. He was eager to ride on a canal boat and see how the canal crossed rivers and climbed up and down hills.

One afternoon invitations came for Darius Lyte, Esquire, and Mistress Amity Lyte. *The Honorable Loammi Baldwin requests the pleasure of your company at a soirée in honor of the Countess of Rumford at half after seven on Saturday evening, August the thirtieth, 1806.*

Amity's heart leaped. An evening party! How long since she had danced? Her mind raced back to the marsh cottage and the Virginia reel. But—would her father let her go?

She watched red stain Darius's neck and forehead, and half expected him to crumple the invitation and throw it into the fireplace. Instead he turned the card in his hands and said, "I doubt that my presence would add to the gaiety of the occasion. I shall decline."

She waited for what seemed interminable minutes while he strode back and forth across the room. She cleared her throat. "Father," she began. Oh, why did her voice have to squeak so?

He stopped. "Yes?" he asked as if he were pulling his thoughts back from a great distance.

She swallowed. "There's that beautiful green satin gown Aunt Keziah had made for me. I've never had a chance to wear it. I'm sure she would be pleased to see it used."

He looked at her as if he were seeing her for the first time. "This is no life for a young girl," he said, "working day after day. I'm sure our aunt would want you to wear the gown—and to this ball especially."

"May I go, then?" she quavered.

"You may," he said. Scarcely able to believe her good fortune, Amity slipped out of the room. In the days that followed she wondered how she could possibly wait until the thirtieth. Tim gave daily reports of preparations at the Baldwin mansion, for he was a frequent visitor there. Mrs. Jephthah Richardson, a cousin who served as housekeeper, was in a tizzy. There would be special ices, syllabubs, flummeries, and other treats. The Countess would arrive the day before the ball, and would remain for a week or ten days. Other important guests were coming, none more welcome than young Loammi and Sam.

When the day of the ball arrived, Amity was so busy that she had little time to look forward to it. A dozen guests demanded her attention. And in the middle of the afternoon she found Joe Beaver standing at the back door, his coat in rags and his body emaciated.

"Joe hungry," he said. "Winter come soon. Joe need food to keep warm." He held out an arm so thin it was little more than bone.

"Sit down and I'll get you something to eat." She filled a plate with cold chicken, boiled beets, and three rolls. As she passed the open door to the shed she saw her father's old coat hanging there. On the nail beside it was the tall beaver hat with its red riband. Darius had not worn either since he had been newly outfitted. Why not give them to Joe Beaver?

She took the filled plate to him, and when he had finished, presented him with the coat and hat. He gave a somber grunt.

"You get drink for Joe?" he asked.

"No drink," she said firmly, "but you may sleep in the barn tonight. Give me your pipe."

He lifted a hand in protest. "No sleep here. Joe smoke now. Then find drink. Sleep there." He pointed down the road. Slowly he shrugged his arms into the coat, set the hat on his lank, greasy hair, and set off with his shuffling gait. There was a pathos in the thin figure. Strangely troubled, she watched him go.

23

Soirée for a Countess

At seven o'clock Sam Baldwin presented himself, resplendent in new russet coat and fawn trousers. Nicole
was placing the last floweret in Amity's chignon when
Tim raced up the stairs with the announcement that
Sam had arrived. Was she ready?

Amity shook out the folds of her pale green satin
gown, smoothed the lace ruching at her neck, and pirou-
etted slowly in her new green slippers. Nicole clapped
her hands in rapturous approval.

Catching up the ivory shawl Aunt Keziah had given
her that afternoon, Amity hurried down the stairs. A
few guests looked up from late dinners to stare at her.

"If you don't look like a princess!" The admiration in
Sam's eyes startled her.

"Don't let the Countess hear you say such a thing,"
Amity warned. "She wouldn't want anyone of higher rank
at a soirée in her honor." She laid her fingers lightly on
the arm Sam extended, and they walked beneath the

rowan tree arch. At the end of the path stood the Baldwin carriage.

"I told Uncle you wouldn't mind walking," said Sam, "but he said dancing slippers were not meant for roads. Besides, he wanted me back in a hurry so I could help receive guests. Sally isn't ready yet, and people will be arriving soon."

The Baldwin mansion was like a buzzing hive. A grayhaired, motherly woman met them at the door, and was introduced as Aunt Jephthah Richardson. She was clasping her fingers together nervously.

"Poor Sally can't seem to get her hair right," she said. "The more she fusses, the worse it looks. Yours looks beautiful. Could you help Sally with hers?"

"I'm sorry, but I have no knack with hair," said Amity. "A friend did mine, a little French girl. Do you think the Countess would like her help?"

Mrs. Richardson's face lit up. "Sam," she said, tapping him on the shoulder, "you jump right back in that carriage and fetch this French person. We've got to get Sally downstairs before the Sullivans arrive."

Sam clucked to the horses, and drove them pounding down the road. Amity waited, looking curiously at the spacious parlors on either side of the large hall. What a beautiful house! Crystal chandeliers hung from gesso ornamented ceilings. Satin damasks were draped about deep windows. Chairs lined walls painted with scenes of the canal, and waxed floors shone with a high gloss. In a corner musicians played tentative notes. The air was heavy with expectancy.

Colonel Baldwin walked toward them from the dining room, flicking a crumb from the lapel of his blue satin coat. "Everything and everyone seems to be ready except Sally," he said, his agitation plain. "Jephthah, you go up and tell her nobody will be looking at her hair."

"That's not a thing to tell a young lady," sputtered the woman. "Besides, here's someone who'll make her presentable." She hurried toward the door and welcomed Nicole, then hurried her up the stairs.

The Colonel disappeared, and Amity was left with Sam and a tall young man whose thatch of hair and strong features made him seem like an older version of Sam.

"This is my cousin Loammi. Don't let him put on airs even though he has designed and built a fire engine for the town of Groton, written a book, and practices law as well."

Amity would have known Loammi as a Baldwin anywhere. He had that special air of disciplined vigor.

"Is your book about fire engines or law?" she asked.

"Neither," said the young man with a laugh. "It's called *Memoirs of Count Rumford.*"

"Could you tell me something about it?"

"It's about his experiments with heat and light," began Loammi, and he launched into a spate of terms so confusing that Amity could hardly understand them. He went on and on, ending, "That's why I admire so greatly Count Rumford's scientific discoveries."

Footsteps sounded on the staircase. There was a swish of skirts, and a head bent over the balustrade. "You are an admirer of Count Rumford's daughter, too, I hope?" Sally Thompson gave him an arch smile.

"You know I've been your admirer ever since you

fished me out of the duck pond when I was a toddler," said Loammi.

The Countess stretched out her arm and tapped him on the head with her fan. "You are horrid to remind me that I'm older than you. Uncle Lambie, scold him."

Did the Colonel wince at the nickname? "Hurry down, Sally," he said. "I want you in the south parlor before the guests come, so we can have a receiving line there with the Sullivans and Judge Parker."

What a heavenly shade of blue the Countess was wearing, with exquisite sprays of pink roses embroidered on the skirt and train. Her blue satin muff was decorated with the same stitchery. Her coiffure was as elegant as her court gown. Nicole had coaxed the thick dark locks into a style that gave needed breadth to the Countess's thin face, and softened her sharp features.

"I am so pleased with my hair that I have half a mind to engage Nicole as my maid," remarked the countess. Amity drew in her breath. A fine way to repay her kindness.

A slight figure tiptoed down the staircase. "Should I go home now?" whispered Nicole.

The Countess whirled around. "Don't think of leaving until the party is over," she ordered. "I may need you to do my hair again."

The Colonel nodded at Nicole. "Yes, do remain. You might ask Mrs. Richardson if she would like you to help serve."

An hour later Amity was dancing with Sam in a quadrille. How handsome he looked, swinging her to the right and to the left with gay vigor.

Then Loammi must have her as his partner. He complimented her upon turning the Lyte homestead into an inn. "You've more than average enterprise. There must be a good brain behind those lovely eyes."

She was so pleased she couldn't reply.

"I admire enterprise," Loammi went on. "I wish I had enough to leave the practice of law and go into civil engineering."

"Wouldn't Sam like to work in engineering, too?" she asked.

"Do you think such work is important?" he countered. "As much so as the ministry or law?"

"Of course. Ministers and lawyers couldn't build a canal."

She must have said the right thing. His face lit up, and he exclaimed, "I wish there were more like you."

When the music stopped he escorted her to a group surrounding the Countess and left her between two gentlemen whom she had met earlier. The one with short curly white hair and twinkling eyes was the Honorable James Sullivan, Attorney General of Massachusetts and President of the Middlesex Canal. The other, far younger but already going bald, was Judge Parker. Chuckling, he said that in this house his being a shareholder in the Middlesex Canal was more important than sitting on the Supreme Judicial Court of Massachusetts.

Sally Thompson was saying, "The Colonel spoils me with such an evening as this, but he knows that I'd rather dance to the music of Woburn fiddlers than attend the grandest opera in Europe."

In the laughter that followed, Amity heard a stifled

bark. The Countess's embroidered muff moved in her lap, and a tiny dog poked out its head.

"You didn't bring the Maltese in here, Sally!" The Colonel's tone was disapproving.

"You know Cora goes everywhere with me," said the Countess, bridling. "When I was visiting President Willard at Harvard I took her to the chapel service. She was very good except during the sermon when she gave one little bark."

"Humph!" snorted the judge.

Sally opened her fan with a quick twist of her wrist. She turned to the Attorney General. "Do you know how to flirt a fan, sir?" she asked, her eyes dancing.

He chuckled, and took the fan from her hand. Opening it, he moved it back and forth before her face. "No, my dear," he said, "but I do know how to fan a flirt!"

Sam appeared then with cups of frothy syllabub. Behind him came waiters bearing trays of delicacies.

During a lull, Judge Parker bent toward Amity. "I understand that you are the daughter of Darius Lyte. He was a limner of the first quality. Has he resumed his work of portraiture?"

"No, not since the death of my mother and brothers."

"A pity to let grief rob the world of his talent, and to deny himself a possible consolation," observed the judge. "There is need for painters of his caliber. I am searching for one now to do the likeness of a man of great accomplishment—our host of this evening." He raised his glass toward the Colonel.

Amity said nothing. Could the judge guess at how impossible such a prospect was?

The musicians filed back to their places and picked up their instruments. The music set feet tapping. Sam bowed before Amity. She rose and they took a few steps toward the lines of dancers. A tall young man in a blue coat blocked their path.

"Ah, Mistress Amity, I had hoped to see you here." Luke Fenwick was as unruffled as if they had never exchanged more than polite pleasantries. "I trust that I may have the privilege of dancing with you later?" He did not wait for an answer, but made his way past them to join Strobo Dix.

"Is he new in Woburn?" asked Sam.

"He's one of the men who tried to buy Aunt Keziah's house. They plan to open their tavern on the first of September."

Sam whistled. "That's the day after tomorrow." He gave her a smile. "Don't look so worried. That frown doesn't go with your dress. Now how about joining this line?"

But they were destined not to dance the Virginia reel that evening. They had just taken their places when suddenly across the hum of chatter burst a thunderous blast.

Windows rattled against their frames. Punch cups met with a sharp tinkle. Chandeliers swayed, their candles throwing eerie arcs across frightened faces.

Echoes of the sound filled the room. Amity could feel her eardrums throbbing. The boom died away, and there was a moment of utter silence. A voice said, "What was that?" A woman screamed. A man swore. People rushed to the windows. By standing on tiptoe Amity could see a blaze piercing the darkness. It was to the south, along the canal. Great heaven—could it be her home? She stared aghast, and gripped Sam's arm. She could feel his muscles tense. He looked at the flames with a calculating eye. "It's not your house," he said.

They watched with horror as the fire leaped up like a blossoming bush. Then Sam let out his breath in a sharp hiss. A man shouted above the babbling voices, "By Jove, it's the new inn, the Dix House!"

There was a sudden hush. Strobo Dix and Luke Fenwick ran for the door. Behind them streamed the men of Woburn, racing for the carriages.

"If Loammi's new fire engine were here, we might have a chance," said Sam. Then he joined the men in their pell-mell rush to the burning inn.

Amity stood near the window, half sick with shock. From the first leap of flame into the sky she had felt again the old horror, the old sorrow. Once more she saw her father heaping their household goods onto the bonfire in the rear of their home. To the old memory was added the anguish of the fire aboard the packet *Rover* and her search through the smoke for her father. She was trembling with apprehension. Superstitious people said that troubles came in threes. Surely this fire could not mean further disaster!

24

24

The Mob

Amity and Nicole hastened along the road among gathering crowds. In front of the Rowan Tree Inn stood Bessie, Nance, the children, and the inn guests, coats thrown over their sleeping attire, their faces lit by the fire.

Darius Lyte met them and drew them up the path. Of the group he was the only one fully clothed. "A terrible thing!" he said, then asked, "Had anyone at the Baldwins' an idea of how the fire started?"

"Not that I heard," said Amity. She was abysmally weary. She wanted to go to her own room and draw the shades to shut out the hated flames that leaped and flickered.

For the next two days there was talk of nothing but the fire. Scores of the curious streamed out from Boston. Every room and bed in the Rowan Tree Inn was filled. On each person's lips was the question: What caused the explosion? All remarked how fortunate it was that neither the proprietor nor the staff were in the building at the time. Only a blackened heap of timbers marked where the tavern had stood. Though the fire fighters had struggled to extinguish the blaze, passing buckets from hand to hand, their efforts were insufficient to combat such a holocaust.

Amity felt genuine sympathy for Strobo Dix and Luke Fenwick. It must be terrible to face such loss of property. She felt sorry, too, that the evening had ended so abruptly. She had not even thanked Sam for escorting her. And in the morning Tim had reported that Sam had gone to Boston late the day before. When would she see him again?

She had too much work to do to moon about idly. Almost before she realized it, the day was over. She lit candles in the parlors where the guests were reading. She put fresh wood on the fires, for the air was chill. A log fell forward with a shower of sparks. She picked up the poker and nudged the wood back onto the andirons.

Through the window she saw a flicker of flame down the road. What could it be? Not another fire, surely. Anything but that.

With the poker still in her hand, she put her face close to the glass and peered out. There were a row of lights; they were moving, approaching. She heard a distant sound that grew with each moment into a confused babble.

Darius Lyte, adding a column of figures at the desk, looked up. "Hark! What's that?" He rose, pulled aside the drapery and looked out. Instantly the color drained from his face.

Across the night air came the hoarse rumble of men's voices. The wavering flames were torches. In seconds the lights grew brighter, the shouts louder. A band of men was advancing, a surging, violent mob.

Amity watched, her heart pounding. In the forefront marched Jedediah Rapp, waving a flaring pine knot. Behind him marched four men bearing a long timber.

An icy tingle set Amity shivering. She clasped her hands together. The palms were wet with fear. Beside her stood her father, his face twisted, the knuckles of his hand white where he gripped the curtain.

From the parlor opposite a traveler said with excitement, "Looks like they're aiming to ride some poor devil out of town on a rail." His voice held a note of barely hidden pleasure.

Nearer swarmed the throng. Terror flew in its vanguard, straight into the room where Darius Lyte and his daughter waited. Amity could feel it closing viselike about her heart. She broke into a cold sweat as the horde swept up the walk between the rowan trees. The fiery knots lit faces ugly with malice. Coarse mouths bawled jeers.

"That Lyte's the one set fire to the new inn!"

"What a dirty way to get more trade for himself!"

"Come out here, you Tory, and we'll fix you!"

Anger flashed through Amity. The fools! How could they think that her father would set fire to the Dix House? Her father who was the soul of gentleness? How could they accuse him of such an act? Furious, she spun around.

"You'd best get away while there's time," she said to Darius, and ran to the hallway. She had her hand on the door knob when a rock crashed through a window and landed on the floor amid a shower of broken glass. A second later she had flung the door wide and was standing on the broad front step, the poker still in her hand. She had never known such fury in her life. Her head was bursting with it.

Waving the poker, she shouted at the top of her lungs, "Stop! Stop! You're making a terrible mistake!"

The torchlit faces swam in a red mist, Jedediah Rapp's among them. She could feel the hatred rising up from their hot eyes and brandished fists. Another rock shattered a window. A clod of earth thudded against a carved pilaster.

"My father is innocent! He had nothing to do with the fire!" she shrieked.

Her voice was drowned out by a tumult of voices. The torches waved closer. The horde had reached the bottom of the steps and were thrusting their blazing lights near her.

"Stand back and let us at him!"

"He's a filthy Tory!"

"We'll ride him out of town!"

Amity took a firm grip on the poker and planted herself in front of the door. Had her father gotten away? Surely he must have gone out through the back by now. If she could just hold the mob off until he could get well away.

Suddenly the door behind her opened, and Darius Lyte stepped out. She looked at him in wonder. He stood proudly erect, his chin lifted, his head high. His face wore a strange, almost supernatural calm.

The babble of shouts died. A hush filled the air.

"My former friends, my old neighbors," began Darius. "Why do you so misjudge me? I am not a Tory, and never was. I had nothing to do with the fire. Can you not—"

A turf struck him on the side of the head, the shouts arose with renewed fervor, and two men charged up the steps and seized Darius by the arms.

"Fools!" He spat out the word, and kicked at them. Amity raised the poker and swung it at the nearest man. It struck him on the shoulder. Before he could lift his arm to strike, she hit him again. Then a giant hand wrenched the poker from her, and steel fingers pinioned her arms behind her.

She shook the hair from her eyes and saw two men hauling her father down the steps. Writhing and kicking, she struggled to free her arms. But she might as well have tried to break iron chains.

A few feet away Darius was resisting like a demon, his long legs kicking out like flails. He twisted and turned and pulled this way and that in fury. Closer and closer he was drawn to the rail.

Voices rang in Amity's ears. Was she imagining it, or were the shouts growing louder? Probably more enraged citizens were joining the mob. She strained her head and struggled to look beyond her captors. A man in front of her shifted his stance, and in one flash Amity caught a glimpse that gave her new heart.

A gang of men armed with shovels and pickaxes were fighting their way through the mob, laying about them to the right and to the left with their tools. In the forefront, planting well-aimed blows, felling men on either side, plowed the massive figure of Bill Trask. And just behind him, using his fists with amazing skill, was Sam Baldwin.

Amity kicked backward with all her strength at the man who held her. Her heel struck his shin with sharp impact.

"You she-devil!" he gasped, and let go of her wrists. She scrambled away from him, and in a minute was at her father's side. Where was her poker? She must have something to fight with. Then she heard a shout louder than the rest. Bill Trask had reached Darius, and with one blow downed his captor.

At that the fighting ceased. Amity looked out across bloodied heads and blackened eyes, and saw Ned, the bank watch, hustling up the path. He had thrown down his bag of straw, and carried his staff like a lance. He was almost crying as he called out, "Am I too late, boys?"

Bill Trask took a stance in front of the steps. He flexed one mighty arm, and brandished his fist. "Gwan home, all of ye," he shouted, "afore we bash yer to mincemeat."

Sullenly the members of the mob picked themselves up and drifted away. The men with shovels and pickaxes moved forward, Sam and Ned at the rear. "Well, boys, we got here in time," said one.

"Not a minute too soon," said Amity.

Darius Lyte was looking about questioningly. His hair stood up in tufts, his stock hung in shreds across his stained shirt, and his coat sported a rip from shoulder to pocket. "To what do we owe this deliverance?" he asked.

"There was a break in the canal down below," said Sam. "The crew had just got it mended, when Ned came running with word of the mob. So we jumped into the hurry-up boat and came along double-quick."

"So fast we mighta washed out the banks in a new

place." A short Irishman thumped his shovel triumphantly on the ground.

"And Bill Trask?" asked Darius.

"He'd come from Charlestown on a packet that tied up for the night below the locks. He was walking along the towpath when I hailed him and he jumped aboard," explained Sam.

"Just in time for a good brawl," said Bill, rubbing his hands together, the knuckles raw.

Amity looked up and saw that each window framed the frightened faces of the inn's guests. The door burst open, and Nance darted down the steps, her arms wide. Bessie and Nicole followed. Behind them trooped the children, with Ebeneezer peeking out of Tim's nightshirt pocket.

At the last a frail figure appeared, a dressing gown clutched about her. Aunt Keziah swayed on the threshold. "You faced up to them, Darius," she said. "How proud I am of you!"

25

A Warrant for Arson

The last guest had boarded the packet boat the following morning when a chaise drew up at the Rowan Tree Inn. Amity watched a short, pudgy man alight and trudge toward her, a folded paper in his hand.

"Is Darius Lyte to home?" he asked without preamble, his small eyes glinting.

When Darius appeared, the man strode up to him, holding out the folded paper. "Darius Lyte, I serve you with this warrant," he said in a loud voice.

Darius stepped back as if he had been struck. "A warrant? In the name of heaven, what for?"

"Arson." The man bit off the word. "I have orders to take you into custody. Will you come peaceable, or do I have to use force?" He put his hand on a pistol stuck into his belt.

Intent on reading the document, Darius made no answer. Then he exclaimed, "Dix and Fenwick think it was I that set fire to their place? Preposterous!"

"All I know," said the constable stubbornly, "is that I

got orders to take you to jail. And I can't wait around all day arguing. Want your girl to get you a change of clothes?"

Amity flew upstairs to her father's room. Hurriedly she packed a valise and gave it to Darius.

"There's nothing that can be proven against me," he said confidently. "I'll probably be back within the hour. Don't worry." He walked indignantly to the chaise. Amity watched him go with a sinking heart.

An hour passed, and Darius Lyte had not returned. Another hour and another. Amity was beside herself with anxiety. It had all happened so quickly! If only he would return before she had to tell Aunt Keziah that he had gone—and where!

Finally she could stand the uncertainty no longer. She had put on her bonnet and was about to set out for the village when a horse stopped in front of the house, and Sam Baldwin swung down from the saddle.

"Uncle is coming later to talk with you about your father," he said. "I came on ahead to tell you that he's been taken to the county jail in Cambridge. I was afraid the mob might try to form again and attack him on the way, but there wasn't a ripple of trouble. I guess they learned their lesson last night."

Amity hardly heard all that he said. Her father in jail. At that point her mind had stopped. It was incredible. Darius Lyte wasn't a person who endangered others and had to be put away.

Colonel Baldwin, when he came, was grim-visaged. He deplored last night's demonstration. Men's evil passions were too easily inflamed, and often without reason.

Had he not retired early he would have made every effort to halt the mob.

"My dear," he continued, "we must not delude ourselves as to the gravity of your father's situation. The warrant for his arrest stated that there was probable cause to believe that he had committed a felony—in his case, arson. You may not know that the penalty for setting fire to a dwelling house in the nighttime is—death."

"Oh, no!" Amity buried her face in her hands. Imprisonment she could understand. But death! Her head swam. Her ears rang, and her sight blurred. Slowly reason returned. If a house were set afire in the nighttime, was it not more than probable that its inhabitants might perish? In a way, arson was a form of murder. But Mr. Dix's tavern had been empty. Would that make a difference in the crime with which her father was charged?

"I am not trying to frighten you, but to help you understand just how serious the charge against your father is. It is so weighty that he cannot be released on bail except by a special order of the Supreme Judicial Court and he would get that only if the circumstances required it. In his case they do not. So he must remain in custody until the Supreme Judicial Court shall sit in Middlesex County the last week in October."

"But that is two months away! Father can't stay in jail for two months!" The thought was insupportable.

"He has no choice," said the Colonel. "At least you can be sure he will be safe from those who might attempt to take justice into their own hands, as they did last night."

Amity drew a deep, shuddering breath. Surely this was a nightmare from which she would soon awaken.

"Now, my dear," continued Colonel Baldwin, "my son Loammi desires to represent your father in court. He is not the most experienced attorney, but he is honest and he is thorough. He will come to see you this evening. You can best help your father by answering all his questions with complete candor. Loammi will want to talk with everyone in the house. Do not trouble yourself about his fee; he wishes to volunteer his services. Are you willing to work with him?"

"Oh, yes!" Amity clasped her hands together earnestly. She looked up at the Colonel. "Sam has told me that you are a Special Justice. Will you be at Father's trial?"

"Not as a judge. I sit only in the Court of Common Pleas, and your father's case will be tried before the Supreme Judicial Court of Massachusetts."

Amity's spirits plunged even lower. Thinking that the Colonel might take part in the trial had given her a few minutes of comfort.

"You have met two of the gentlemen who will take important parts in the proceedings," he said. "Surely you have not forgotten Mr. James Sullivan, Attorney General for Massachusetts, who was at the soirée for Sally. And Isaac Parker, who was also there, will be one of the justices at the trial. They are both known for their integrity and fair judgment."

No one could ask for more than integrity and fair judgment. Amity could feel a little lessening of the strain. Surely her father's innocence could be proven.

"Now let us go and talk with your aunt. There is nothing we older folk dislike more than being kept in the dark." The Colonel rose and gestured Amity toward Aunt Keziah's room.

Early in the evening young Loammi Baldwin came, his brown eyes thoughtful and his face solemn. "I want to talk with every person here who saw your father the night of the fire," he said.

Their reports were what she had expected. Aunt Keziah had retired early. Nance and Bessie had spent the evening in the kitchen, drinking raspberry shrub and talking, after the children had gone to bed. Mr. Lyte had worked on the accounts, they said, and then had gone for a walk. He usually took an evening stroll.

The young lawyer nodded. "That all fits in with what Mr. Lyte told me. Did anyone see him when he came back?"

"Not until after the explosion. Then we all ran from our beds and met in the front hallway," said Bessie.

"You had all retired and were in your night gear?"

"Yes."

"Even Mr. Lyte?"

Bessie paused. She looked toward Nance. "No, he was dressed," she admitted.

"If he had retired, would he have had time to put on his clothing?"

"Oh no, we got down in double-quick time."

"Then he might possibly have gone to the Dix House and set some explosive charge during the period when you did not actually see him?"

Bessie's face turned purple. "You know he wouldn't do no such thing," she stormed. "Not Mr. Darius."

"But how many people believe in him as you do? Jedediah Rapp has sworn that he saw Darius Lyte entering the Dix House shortly before the fire broke out." Loammi shook his head in discouragement. "All we have is Mr. Lyte's word that he was out walking on the tow-path."

There was a moment's hush.

"Can any of you think of anything that happened that day that was in any way unusual?" The lawyer looked around the circle of faces.

Amity thought back over the busy hours of August thirtieth. "Joe Beaver came," she said uncertainly. "I gave him some supper and some old clothes of Father's. He didn't stay to sleep in our barn, but said he wanted to smoke and find a drink."

Loammi paid little heed. "That old Indian is always bothering people," he said shortly.

When the others had left, Loammi asked, "Have you any family papers, anything that might indicate that your father was not a Loyalist? Even though he is being tried for another matter, I suspect that the jury's feelings will undoubtedly be swayed by their suspicions. If I could prove that he was friendly to the cause of liberty, they might be more impartial in their decision."

The old accusation again. Amity sighed heavily. "Everything we brought from New York was burned on the *Rover*," she said. "The only papers I know of in this house are Continental bills in the old Bible box. Would you like to see them?" She unlocked the cupboard and took down the box. As she turned the key and lifted the lid, she recalled her first glimpse of it. How changed everything was from that time! She lifted a handful of bills and riffled them. "See?" she said to Loammi. "All Continental money, every single piece, and not worth the paper it's printed on. If it weren't for your father's help, Aunt Keziah would be in the almshouse."

"He only did what seemed right to him." Loammi dismissed the matter. "Let's see how much there is," he said, picking up a sheaf of bills. "That would give us an idea of how heavily your aunt invested in the Continental cause."

"Would that help Father?"

"It would prove that one member of the family had faith in the cause of liberty." He began counting. "Sixteen hundred dollars here. What's this packet at the bottom? Oho! It looks different."

He held it out for Amity's inspection. A long strip of paper was folded about a bundle of notes. On it was written: *Property of Darius Lyte.* Inside were more pieces of currency. Loammi spread them out. "Good Lord!" he said. "There's ten thousand dollars here. Your father must have put his entire inheritance into the support of the Continental Army."

Ten thousand dollars! Regret swept over Amity. If only they could have some of it now. They'd not have to take in guests; there would be money enough to repay Colonel Baldwin, and enough to pay this young lawyer's fee.

"Is it worth anything?"

"I'm afraid not," he said. "It has no monetary value. However, I'll take it along as evidence. You've no objection?"

She hardly noticed what he was doing, she was so discouraged and fearful. Everything looked absolutely hopeless. Who would believe her father's word against that of Jedediah Rapp? Nothing short of a miracle could save him. She could feel tears starting, and shut her eyes. But they collected beneath her lids and ran down her cheeks.

Loammi patted her on the shoulder. "Try not to worry," he urged. "Your father will have a fair trial."

A fair trial! All through the night Amity tossed and turned, tortured by thoughts of her father in jail. What must be his fears? His anguish? At last she rose and by candlelight wrote a letter to Mlle. Armand. Relieved to have shared her problem, she went back to bed and at last slept.

26

"God send you a good deliverance!"

A week later Mlle. Armand stepped off the packet. The minute she was inside the door, Amity clung to her helplessly, her self-control all at once dissolved.

"*Chérie*, you have had much to bear alone," said the Frenchwoman, stroking Amity's hair. "Let yourself cry; it will do you good."

Amity lifted her head. "It's so terrible to have him locked up," she sobbed. "Every time I step outside the door I think of Father, and that he cannot—"

"I feel the same," said Mlle. Armand. "It hurts me." She put one hand to her heart. For a few minutes she held Amity close. Then she said briskly, "Come now, I shall put away my things. And then you will show me what I may do to help. I am going to remain with you until your father returns."

Her words gave Amity hope. With Mlle. Armand's help she managed to endure the long weeks that followed.

The Frenchwoman took over the inn's accounts, her neat columns of figures untangling intricacies that had baffled Amity and Darius. She advised Bessie about menus, showing her how to make omelets, and salads with a dressing of oil and vinegar. In the evening she often read aloud to the children.

September passed. October began. The rowanberries hung in crimson clusters. Baldwin apples ripened, firm and crisp. With the cool weather came a decline in the number of guests, and Amity was not sorry. Her enthusiasm for innkeeping had waned. She saw it now only as a means of survival, and without regret watched the others turning more and more to Mlle. Armand for direction.

Bill Trask elected to remain in Woburn with his family after returning briefly to Boston to sell his hackney coach and mare. He chopped wood, laid fires, carried luggage, and cared for the lawn and gardens.

As the time for the trial drew near, Amity's anxiety increased. Twice she and Mlle. Armand journeyed to Cambridge to see Darius in the Sunday afternoon visiting hours, taking fresh clothing and a basket of Bessie's good food.

Again Loammi Baldwin came to the inn to talk with Amity. Once more he asked her to recount her actions on August thirtieth. Perhaps unwittingly she had overlooked some important point. She told him again of Joe Beaver's visit. This time the young lawyer listened intently.

"What clothes did you give him?" he asked.

"Just an old coat and a beaver hat Father wore the day we came to Aunt Keziah's. The hat had a red riband."

Loammi clapped a fist into his open palm. "That's it!" he cried. "Jed Rapp must have seen Joe Beaver wearing your father's clothes. Joe is tall and thin. In the dim light he might have looked like your father."

Amity's spirits swung upward.

"All we have to do is find Joe Beaver," said Loammi. "Though if he did go near the tavern that night, it's not likely he would want to admit it." He paused, and a musing look crossed his face. "I wonder," he said, "if Joe was the one—"

But though Loammi sought diligently, he could not locate the Indian. No one seemed to know where he had gone. It was as if he had disappeared into the air.

Finally, the last week in October arrived. On Monday morning Loammi called on Amity. "The Supreme Judicial Court meets tomorrow to try cases arising in the County of Middlesex," he said. "A grand jury will be chosen, and will consider the indictment against your father. Undoubtedly they will think there is enough evidence so that he ought to be tried, and will return 'a true bill.' He must then be arraigned before three justices."

"I want to be with him," said Amity, her heart pounding.

"There's no point in your being there tomorrow," said Loammi. "But you may wish to be present on Wednesday for the arraignment. Quite possibly the trial will commence the following day."

On Tuesday Amity and Mlle. Armand boarded the packet for Charlestown. Bessie, Nance, Bill, and Nicole bade them a tearful farewell. They were not even to think about the inn, the children, or Aunt Keziah.

The day was dark and dull, with gusts of penetrating damp. Amity and Mlle. Armand sat inside the cabin, silently watching the landscape slide past the windows.

Today's trip couldn't be more of a contrast to her first journey on the canal a year ago, thought Amity. How bright had been her anticipation! How keen her enjoyment as they passed through lock and aqueduct. Now she could barely rouse from her gloom to note the packet's progress.

From Charlestown they went directly to Green Street in Boston. Amity had written to Mrs. Snow about lodgings, and the schoolmistress had replied that they must not consider going anywhere but her house. She was taking fewer pupils; there was ample room, and the courthouse was but a short ride across the Charles and down Broadway to Harvard Square.

Loammi Baldwin met them at the courthouse door Wednesday morning. "Do not be disturbed at questions Mr. Sullivan may ask," he told Amity. "Remember, it is the duty of the Attorney General to protect the state and its people by convicting criminals so that they may be placed where they can do no more harm."

Amity and Mlle. Armand followed him to the high-vaulted courtroom, and sat on a wooden bench near the front. For a few minutes Amity was aware only of the thudding of her heart. Then she looked about at the people filling the benches, and at the officials in the front section of the room.

Colonel Baldwin entered, and was immediately greeted by a score of men. Behind him came Sam, his eyes searching the room. He walked straightway to where she sat, and took a place at her side. Just having him near was strengthening.

There was a stir in the courtroom. The people rose and remained silent while the four judges entered and took

their places. Garbed in flowing black robes, they seemed
to Amity like four figures of doom. Then she studied
their faces.

The Chief Justice, Theophilus Parsons, walked with
rapid steps, his lean face with its scraggly brows filled
with kindly concern. Behind him came Samuel Sewall
and Theodore Sedgwick, their features intent as if they
were already weighing facts. The fourth justice she recognized from Colonel Baldwin's party. With his dimpled
chin and fair complexion, Isaac Parker looked young for
his weighty responsibilities. A solemn hush prevailed.
There was no doubt as to the awesome dignity of the
state's Supreme Court.

Prisoners were brought in, one by one, for a brief
period while their indictments were read. Amity scarcely
heard a word. She was looking for one beloved face,
listening for one terrifying indictment.

Then Darius Lyte's name was called, and he was led
into the room. How straight and tall he was. And how
distinguished. Amity looked more closely. There was
something different about him. He seemed to have undergone an inner change. His eyes, deep-set and circled,
looked out from his white face with a strange serenity.
Even from where she sat, Amity could tell that the inward shadow was gone.

At an order the clerk rose and began to read: "The
jurors for the Commonwealth of Massachusetts upon their
oath present that Darius Lyte, Esquire, of Woburn in
the County of Middlesex, not having the fear of God
before his eyes, but being moved and seduced by the
instigation of the Devil on the thirtieth day of August
in the present year of our Lord one thousand eight

hundred and six at Woburn in the County of Middlesex aforesaid did wilfully and maliciously set fire to the tavern known as the Dix House according to sworn testimony given by Jedediah Rapp, Yeoman, of Woburn, that he did see the accused enter said tavern on the night of the thirtieth of August aforesaid after which a conflagration did violently break out—"

The clerk's voice went on, punctuating its utterance with legal phraseology. Amity's head swam. At last the clerk paused, then asked, "Darius Lyte, what say you to this indictment? Are you guilty or not guilty?"

"Not guilty," the prisoner answered firmly.

"How will you be tried?" asked the clerk.

"By God and my country." The prescribed phrase took on a new meaning as he spoke it.

"God send you a good deliverance!" said the clerk.

A good deliverance. The words repeated themselves over and over again in Amity's mind. If only God might truly send her father a good deliverance! She could feel her whole being concentrated in a prayer that justice would prevail and her father's innocence be proven.

Darius Lyte was remanded, and the business of the court went on. At length adjournment was announced. Court would reconvene the next day at nine o'clock, and would consider first the case of Darius Lyte.

Amity was hardly conscious of the intervening hours. She lifted food to her lips, but could not taste it. She went for a long walk with Mlle. Armand, but scarcely knew that her feet were moving. All night she lay wakeful and worried.

And like one caught in an evil spell, she entered the courtroom again, and watched her father brought in by a guard. She listened numbly while the jurors were sworn, promising well and truly to try, and true deliverance to make, between the Commonwealth of Massachusetts and the prisoner, according to the evidence.

With unbelieving ears she heard the Solicitor General inquire of each juror, "Have you any conscientious scruples of sitting in a case of life and death, or do you believe it unlawful to take human life by law?" With the same unbelief she heard them reply in the negative.

Then the clerk rose. "Gentleman of the Jury," he said, "hearken to an indictment found by the grand inquest for the body of the County of Middlesex against the prisoner at the bar." Once more he read the dreadful accusation. "To this indictment," he continued, "the prisoner at the bar has pleaded not guilty and for trial has put himself on God and the country; which country you are; and you are now sworn to try the issue. If he is guilty, you will say so; if he is not guilty, you will say so and no more. Good men and true, stand together and hearken to your evidence."

Amity studied the twelve men on the jury. Some were old, some young. Some had thick features, some fine hewn. But each one wore an expression of deep responsibility. It was clear they felt themselves truly to represent the country in trying this man. She wondered if any of them were from Woburn. If so, would their minds be infected with the poison of suspicion that Darius Lyte had been disloyal to the American cause during the Revolution?

The case was opened by the Solicitor General with a speech impressing upon the jurors the solemnity of their task. "If the evidence against Darius Lyte shall be suf-

214 / THE LIMNER'S DAUGHTER

ficient to satisfy you of his guilt, the laws of God and your country sentence him to a vile and ignominious death.

"So that you may have a correct understanding of this case, I will read to you from Chapter 131 of the Laws and Resolves of Massachusetts for the year 1804, an Act providing for the punishment of incendiaries and the perpetrators of other malicious mischiefs.

"Section one. Be it enacted by the Senate and House of Representatives in General Court assembled, and by the authority of the same that if any person shall wilfully and maliciously set fire to the dwelling house of another or to any outbuilding adjoining to such dwelling house or to any other building and by the kindling of such fire or by the burning of such other building, such dwelling house shall be burnt, in the night time, every such offender and any person present aiding, abetting, or consenting in the commission of such offense or accessory thereto, before the fact, by counselling, hiring, or procuring the same to be done, who shall be duly convicted before the Supreme Judicial Court of either of the felonies and offenses aforesaid shall suffer the penalty of death."

Death. The word seemed to hang over the courtroom like a suffocating pall. Amity found it difficult to breathe.

The Solicitor General continued, "I shall now call the witnesses to prove the facts."

Jedediah Rapp was first called upon to testify. His moon face was flushed, and his eyes darted from side to side.

Mr. James Sullivan rose. Stern and solemn, he looked every inch the Attorney General, his blue eyes piercing beneath his crisp white hair. Could this awesome figure be the courtly guest who had gaily told the Countess at the Colonel's party that he knew how to fan a flirt?

"You have previously stated that you saw Darius Lyte on the evening of August thirtieth. Will you please to tell the gentlemen of the jury about that occurrence in detail?"

Mr. Rapp ran his tongue over his lips. "About ten o'clock at night I was walking up the road when I saw Darius Lyte coming from the opposite direction. He went up on the side porch of the new tavern, pushed open the door, and walked in."

"How could you tell it was Mr. Lyte?"

"There was a full moon that night. I couldn't mistake him. I've known that Tory a good many years."

Tory! Amity flinched. As one man, the jurors turned to look at Darius Lyte. As one, their expressions betrayed suspicion.

Loammi Baldwin jumped to his feet. "I move that the witness's remark be stricken from the record. We are not trying this man for his political opinions years ago, but for an alleged criminal action last summer."

Judge Parsons regarded him gravely. "The objection is sustained. The jury will disregard the witness's remark, and the witness will confine himself to the events of last August."

The Attorney General addressed Jedediah Rapp. His face was calm, but there was a chill in his voice. "Do you have anything further to testify?"

"I guess not," said Rapp grudgingly.

The judge turned to Loammi Baldwin. "Do you wish to examine this witness?"

"Yes, your honor." The young lawyer turned to Jedediah. "Mr. Rapp, may I ask where you spent the evening

prior to the time you saw the person you thought was
Mr. Lyte?"

"At Warren's Tavern."

"Did you partake of any spirituous liquor there?"

Rapp bristled. "No more than two noggins of flip."

"Then you started home, and when you were near the
Dix House you saw someone approaching. What did you
do then?"

"I hid behind a tree and watched him."

"How far away were you?" pursued Loammi.

"About the breadth of this room."

"Did you speak with him?"

Rapp gave a snort of disdain. "Not likely. Lyte's not
one to talk."

"Were you watching him continually?"

"Not when he was close by. I kept behind the tree
then so he wouldn't see me." A cunning look crossed
Rapp's face.

"How could you see him well enough to identify him
then?"

"I stepped out from behind the tree when he went up
on the side porch."

"Could you see his face?"

"No, his back was toward me."

"How could you identify him if you couldn't see his
face?"

"By his clothes," said Rapp contemptuously. "I'd know
that brown coat with the black velvet collar anywhere.
And that tall hat with the red band. He wore them the
day he came back to Woburn and walked past my shop."

"How many times have you seen Darius Lyte since that
day?"

"Not one. He never comes out of his house to mix with decent people."

Judge Parsons rapped with his gavel. "The witness will not express opinions."

Two bright spots of color burned in Loammi's cheeks. "In other words," he said, "you saw a person wearing clothes that you recognized as having once been worn by Darius Lyte. That is all, thank you."

Jedediah Rapp stumped back to his place angrily, his mouth moving. As he passed near Amity she heard him mutter, "The judge ought to have heard Ben Thompson tell about Lyte's spying for the British. He'd know then that Lyte is a Tory."

Amity's heart almost stopped beating. So Ben Thompson had been the first to point the finger of suspicion at Darius Lyte. His false accusation had put into motion the series of events that had placed her father in jeopardy. The revelation was too devastating to contemplate. She gave a low sob. How she hated that Count Rumford!

But she must concentrate on the trial. The name of Strobo Dix was called. He stepped forward, his hooded lids and beaked nose giving him the look of an eagle.

"You are acquainted with the prisoner?" inquired James Sullivan.

"Yes, I met him at his place about a year ago."

"Was that the only time you had a conversation with him?"

"No," said Strobo Dix. "I met him one day on the road to Woburn. He told me then that he was broke and worried sick about competition from my tavern."

Amity sat up with a jerk. What an unlikely story! Anyone who knew her father would know that Strobo Dix was lying. Darius Lyte would never admit to being low in funds, and he would certainly not say that he feared competition. That he would speak thus to Strobo Dix whom he had scarcely met was the most unlikely part. She glared at the man in the witness stand. He had lifted his chin, and was gazing at the jury with an air of martyrdom. What did he mean, lying like that about her father? She would like to wring his wrinkled neck!

Her eyes flew to the white-faced man in the prisoner's box. Now she knew with desperate finality that her father was indeed on trial for his life, and against the forces of evil. She must not allow fear to dull her mind, but must fight her way out of the miasma of nightmare unreality. If she were to help, she would need every faculty of mind and spirit.

An idea was buzzing around in her head like the fly that was beating its wings against one of the courtroom windows. The thought eluded her. If she could only catch hold of it. She looked at Sam, and then remembered. That afternoon on the canal—what had he said as he rowed the boat past the marsh? Something about his cousins making a magic fire? A sudden possibility struck her. She turned and whispered to Sam. He listened attentively, then rose and tiptoed to Loammi, and the two conferred.

Judge Parsons addressed Loammi. "Do you wish to question the witness?"

Loammi faced the judge. "I do, your honor," he said. Was Amity imagining the note of determination in his voice?

"You were absent from the tavern the evening of the fire, Mr. Dix?" inquired Loammi.

"Yes, Mr. Fenwick and I went out, and the staff was not expected to take up residence until the following day."

"Mr. Dix, was the cellar of your tavern floored over?"

Two of the jurors shot curious glances at the young lawyer. What was he driving at with this talk of a cellar?

"No, we just had a few planks laid down to walk on."

"The floor was of earth?"

"Yes."

"And the section set off to contain your wine and spirits had tight board walls?"

"Yes, it had a heavy door, too. I aimed to get a strong lock for it."

"It was not locked that night?"

"No. The locks I had ordered had not come."

"Then it is possible that someone could have found his way into the cellar and into the wine closet?"

"Yes."

"Now, Mr. Dix, you have stated that you had a conversation with Mr. Lyte one day. Can you tell us exactly what day?"

"About a month before the fire."

"In the morning or afternoon?"

"Er–er–it was the morning."

"What time in the morning?"

"About nine o'clock, I guess."

"And just where did you meet Mr. Lyte?"

"About halfway to the village."

"Surely you can locate the spot more exactly."

"Let's say it was in front of the Wrights' house."

"And you stood in the road and talked at nine in the morning. Do you usually walk to the village?"

"Sometimes I drive my chaise."

"Isn't it correct that you almost always drive in your chaise?"

"That day I was walking." Dix's chin jutted out belligerently.

"What was your reason for being on the road that day?"

"I'd gone to get some supplies."

"And they were?"

"I don't exactly remember. Oh, yes—some nails, that's what it was, a keg of nails."

"And you were going to carry them back to the tavern, a distance of a mile, in your arms? That's a heavy load, Mr. Dix." Loammi paused. The jurors were eyeing Strobo Dix with something less than confidence. "You were on your way to the village?"

"Yes, I was."

"Then Darius Lyte was returning from the village. Wasn't that a rather unusual occurrence? Mr. Rapp has testified that Mr. Lyte rarely left his home."

Strobo Dix let his heavy lids droop. "I guess I was mistaken," he said. "I was on my way back to the tavern from the village."

"Carrying the keg of nails," said Loammi gravely.

"Yes. That is, no," Strobo Dix stammered.

"If Mr. Lyte was on his way to the village, someone else must have seen him," pursued Loammi.

"Lyte must have changed his mind and gone home again," said Dix angrily. "All I know is that we met and he told me he hadn't a cent and that I'd better think twice before opening my tavern or he'd do something to prevent it."

The young attorney fixed Strobo with a gimlet eye. "You stated before that Mr. Lyte was worried about possible competition. Now you say he threatened you. Exactly which statement did he make?"

"He said both things."

"It seems strange that you should remember the second part just now, especially when you seem so unclear about the time and place and direction in which you both were going," said Loammi. "That is all, thank you."

Strobo Dix stepped down with a disgruntled air, his beak and hooded eyes giving him more than ever the look of an eagle. Or of a vulture, Amity amended.

In the brief pause, she turned to Loammi. "Why don't they give my father a chance to tell his story?" she asked, her cheeks burning. "If the jury could just hear him, they'd know he was telling the truth."

"I'd call on him if I could," said the attorney, "but a defendant cannot testify in his own trial, because he has an interest in the outcome. It is a foolish rule, and will some day be abolished, I think, but there is no doubt about its being a law in Massachusetts right now."

"What can we do?" entreated Amity. "Mr. Dix was lying. I know he was. Yet the jury will believe him."

"Perhaps not," said Loammi. "Now pay attention. Another witness is being called."

Luke Fenwick made his way to the stand, his blond hair smooth and his face composed. Not once did he look in her direction. How did he fit into the picture? Amity wondered.

Mr. Sullivan regarded him with an impartial gaze. "You are employed by Mr. Strobo Dix, the owner of the tavern that was recently destroyed?"

"Yes."

"Please tell the court anything you know that may throw light upon this case."

"Early in the spring Mr. Lyte's daughter came past our tavern. She said she was going to turn her aunt's house into an inn, and she didn't act too pleased to hear that Mr. Dix was building a tavern so near. I offered to buy her place. She declined, and I suggested I might be a partner in her inn so she could have the benefit of my experience. She refused and got angry. She told me she had a secret that would ensure her success."

"Did she give you any clue as to this secret?"

"No, but I'm sure she meant then to blow up our place."

Judge Parsons rapped with his gavel. "No conjectures, please."

Amity was boiling with rage. What did Luke Fenwick mean by such an allegation? Furious, she started to jump to her feet. Sam put his hand on her arm and drew her back.

"Does the counsel for the defense wish to cross-examine?"

"Yes, thank you," said Loammi, taking a place near the stand.

"How long have you known Miss Lyte?" he asked Luke.

"About a year," was the response. "We met on the canal packet."

"Did you meet any other members of the Lyte family then?"

"Only her little brother. I rescued him off the roof just as the boat was going under a bridge."

He would have to mention that, thought Amity. She could hear a murmur of approval from the jury box.

"Did you see Miss Lyte between your first meeting and the one you described previously?"

"Yes. Mr. Dix and I called at her home. We offered to buy the house. But the old lady wouldn't sell."

"By 'old lady' you mean?"

"The girl's aunt, Mrs. Woods."

"Why did you think the house might be for sale?"

"We'd heard around town that Lyte was broke. If you could have seen him and his children that day on the packet, you'd have known they didn't have a cent to their names—clothes threadbare, shoes worn through, no luggage. I've never laid eyes on three sorrier specimens—poor but proud. The boy let on that the girl was going to inherit the house, and I thought she might be persuaded to work on the old—on Mrs. Woods to sell it."

Amity bit her lip in fury. So that was why Luke had invited her to go out driving!

The judge was speaking. "Have you finished, Mr. Baldwin?" At Loammi's assent, Judge Parsons asked the Attorney General if he had any more witnesses.

"No more," said Mr. Sullivan.

"Does Mr. Baldwin wish to call any witnesses?"

"Yes," he answered immediately. "I should like to call on Mistress Amity Lyte."

Amity rose on trembling feet. It was all she could do to walk the short distance from her bench to the witness stand. Before her the faces of jurors and spectators swam in a haze.

"Miss Lyte," said Loammi, "can you tell the jurors where you reside?"

"I live in my aunt's home in Woburn."

"Will you tell them something about it?"

"The house is very old and beautiful," she said. "It was built by one of my ancestors. My grandfather added a new portion on the front which is quite large. We use it as an inn now."

"How long has it been used as an inn?"

"Just since this spring."

"Who thought of the idea?"

"I'm afraid I did. It seemed the only way I could help out and still take care of my aunt and my little brother."

"What work does your father perform as innholder?"

"He greets the guests, assigns them rooms, and carries their luggage upstairs. In the evenings he takes care of the accounts and remains at his desk to answer questions or be of help to anyone. And in the morning he carries down the luggage and takes in the fees for the nights' lodging and meals."

"How much time does that involve?"

"Until the last guest has gone. Some don't leave till ten or eleven, depending on which packet they're taking."

"Then it would be very unusual for your father to leave the inn in the morning?"

"My father hasn't been away from the inn in the morning since we opened. I know, because I've been there every day, too." Amity could feel a flush creeping into her cheeks. She looked earnestly at the jury. They must believe her! They must!

"You come from a family of considerable means, Miss Lyte. How does it happen that your house is now used as an inn?"

"My father suffered financial reverses."

"Is it not true that he inherited the sum of ten thousand dollars from his parents?"

"I believe so."

"Why do you not live upon that money?"

"My father invested it years ago. The investment—" What could she say? Certainly not that he had made a poor investment, or that it had failed!

"Isn't it true that he put the entire sum into Continental currency? Do you recognize these certificates as his property?" Loammi held aloft the bundle of money wrapped in the paper bearing Darius Lyte's name.

Among the spectators a man exclaimed. "Ten thousand dollars in Continental money! Lord!"

"Yes, that is his property," said Amity.

"What was your father's purpose in using his inheritance thus?"

"Our country needed the money to supply its troops, so he gave all that he had." It was as simple as that.

"He wished to support the cause of liberty, Miss Lyte. Is that true?"

"Of course." What other reason could there be?

Amity had been so absorbed in replying to Loammi's questions she had hardly looked at the jury. Now she could see the change in their faces. They were looking at her father with a new expression. The suspicion and distrust were gone. In their place were a new respect, and yes—a kind of admiration. Not every man had ten thousand dollars' worth of devotion to his country!

"Can you tell us about your conversation with Mr. Fenwick?"

Amity could feel her anger returning. She clenched her jaw. She must keep her temper at all costs. "What he said is true. He did offer to buy our house, and when we refused he asked to go into business with us. But I didn't want his help. I thought we could manage by ourselves."

"What was the secret you referred to?"

"It was silly of me to say that," confessed Amity. "What I meant was Bessie's wonderful cooking. I didn't think any other inn could provide meals to equal hers."

"The secret you referred to was your cook's skill?"

"Yes." Amity wished the jurors wouldn't laugh. It was true. Bessie was a superb cook.

The judge was pounding with his gavel. Did she imagine a twitch at the corners of his mouth? Then Loammi was questioning her again.

"Miss Lyte, can you tell us anything about your father's whereabouts the night of the fire?"

"I wasn't at home." It wouldn't be proper to mention the party, she thought.

"Did you see your father when you returned home?"

"Yes."

"What was he wearing?"

"The same suit he has on now."

Loammi looked at her earnestly. "Miss Lyte, has your father ever owned a coat and hat similar to those described by Mr. Rapp?"

"Yes—a tall hat with a red band, and a brown coat with a black velvet collar. He wore them the day we arrived."

"Has he worn them since?"

"Only the first few days we were here. Then the tailor made him two new suits, and the old one was discarded."

"What happened to the old coat and hat?"

"I gave them to an Indian named Joe Beaver the day of the fire."

"What did he do with them?"

"He put them on and went away."

"Did he say where he was going?"

"Not exactly." Amity hesitated. "After I gave him his supper, he asked for a drink—of liquor. I wouldn't give him one, but I said he could sleep in the barn if he wanted, and told him to give me his pipe and flint and steel. We always did that for fear he might set the barn on fire. He said he did not want to sleep in our barn. He wanted to get a drink and smoke his pipe. So he went off."

"In which direction did he go?"

"Toward the Dix House."

"Wearing your father's hat and coat?

"Yes."

"That will be all, thank you," said Loammi, "unless the Attorney General wishes to examine you." He looked toward James Sullivan, who said he had no questions.

"I wish to call one more witness, if it please your honor," said Loammi. "Mr. Edward Bumpus."

Amity looked up in surprise. Who in the world was Edward Bumpus? A moment later she caught her breath in surprise. Ned, the bank watchman for the canal, strangely unfamiliar in a tight coat and long white stock askew under his ragged beard, lumbered to the stand.

After Ned had been sworn in and had stated his occupation, Loammi asked, "Can you tell us anything as to the whereabouts of the prisoner on the night of August thirtieth?"

"That I can," said Ned. "There was a full moon that night, and I was walking along the towpath keeping my eyes sharp. Them musquashes come out after sundown, and I was after one big fellow that had dug too many danged holes in my banks. I had just found a fresh hole, and was in the water plugging it up when Mr. Lyte come along."

"How did you know it was Mr. Lyte?"

"I've knowed him since he was a boy and tried to talk me out of snaring rabbits. Said they didn't do no harm."

"Had you and Mr. Lyte had any conversation recently?"

"Nope. He never said a word to no one since he come back, far as I know. That night he just walked along the way he always did, his hands behind his back."

"How was he dressed?"

"I didn't notice nothing special. Just a white shirt and dark coat and his head bare. He never wore a hat that I saw."

"Where was Mr. Lyte at the time you described?"

"Near a quarter of a mile above Colonel Baldwin's place."

"What time was it?"

"Pretty late. Mr. Lyte had just passed, going toward the Colonel's and his own house, when I heard the explosion. Scared me so I fell back into the water. When I got up I could see Darius streaking down the path toward his house on those long legs of his'n. I took out after him, but I couldn't keep up."

A whispering arose in the courtroom. Amity could see the eyes of the jurors widen at Ned's testimony.

"One more thing, Mr. Bumpus," continued Loammi.

"You have known the prisoner for many years, since he was a boy, in fact. Did Darius Lyte ever to your knowledge give aid to the British?"

"Him that's the soul of honor? Not on your life! I guess you don't know Darius or you wouldn't ask me that!" sputtered Ned.

The courtroom was filled with a buzz of talk as spectators exclaimed to one another.

The Attorney General raised his voice. "Your honor, I object."

Judge Parsons hammered with his gavel. "The objection is sustained. The jury will disregard the witness's remarks. The foregoing question and reply will be stricken from the record."

When quiet again prevailed, Loammi addressed Judge Parsons. "I would beg that the jury be taken to Woburn to view the scene of the crime."

"I trust that your reason is of sufficient importance to justify such a move," said the judge.

"It is vitally necessary for the implementation of justice," said Loammi.

"Very well. You will come to my chambers and there inform the Attorney General and myself exactly what evidence you propose to produce, and your reasons for so doing."

27

The Verdict

On returning to Boston, Amity found Mrs. Snow's house in a hubbub. The countess had arrived that afternoon from a visit to her grandmother in Windham, and was regaling Mrs. Snow with detailed accounts of what she had been doing. Pleading a headache, Amity escaped to her room. The headache was real enough, and after Mr. Rapp's disclosure of Ben Thompson's accusation of her father, she could not bear Sally's frivolities.

Stretched on her bed, her fingers to her throbbing temples, Amity fell into an exhausted sleep. It was dark when she awoke, refreshed, but weak with hunger. Lighting a candle, she tiptoed downstairs and made her way to the buttery. She found milk and bread and cold ham, and was carrying a tray to her room when a door in the upstairs hall opened, and the Countess peered out. In her dressing gown, with her hair down her back, she looked younger and somehow defenseless.

"Can't you sleep either?" she asked Amity. "Come in and talk to me."

Amity hesitated. Talk was the last thing she wanted at that moment, especially with the daughter of the blackguard who had falsely accused her father. But there was a loneliness in the young woman's eyes that she could not ignore. She stepped reluctantly into the room.

Open trunks and boxes stood about, spilling over with frilly petticoats and silk gowns. The Countess cleared a portion of the crowded desk. "You can put your tray here. I was writing a letter to my father, but it can wait."

To her father. The words cut at Amity like a poniard. She burst into angry tears. The Countess's father was far away, famous, and free from the jeopardy in which Darius was pinioned. Amity was about to lash out at Sally Thompson. She wanted to inflict some hurt on the daughter of the man who had brought such pain to her family.

Sally put a hand on Amity's shoulder. Involuntarily Amity jerked away. "Forgive me," said Sally sadly, as if rejection were no stranger to her. "I'm always saying the wrong thing. That's what I'm trying to write to him about, what steps I'm taking to improve myself." She pointed to a pile of correspondence. "Those are all scolding letters—how I hate them! He's always trying to make me over! He doesn't want a daughter. He wants a perfect specimen of manners he can show off to society as the product of his training—just as if I were one of his scientific experiments!"

Amity listened in amazement, her tears forgotten.

"Does your father point out your faults to you?" demanded the Countess. She did not wait for a reply. "You should have seen my father's rage when he took me to call on a baroness and I curtsied to the housekeeper!

He was so mortified he wouldn't speak to me for a week!"

"Father doesn't pay much attention to what I do," said Amity.

"But he must care for you. He didn't run off and desert you and your mother as my father did when I was a baby," declared the Countess passionately. "When I was young and needed a father's love, I never heard from him. Once I was grown, he suddenly sent for me and tried to make me over. Sometimes I almost hate him. Why can't he love me as I am?" She marched up and down the room, kicking at hatboxes and valises. "The worst thing is that whenever a man shows any interest in me, or Father thinks I'm attracted to him, he separates us. It's true! It's happened time and again." Sally's voice broke. "I'll never be able to get married!"

Jolted out of her own troubles, Amity was torn between surprise and sympathy. To think she had envied Sally! The poor thing had more reason to hate Count Rumford than she—and the Count her own father! Amity's anger dissolved, and she did her best to comfort the unhappy young woman.

The next morning Amity and Mlle. Armand, by special permission of Justice Parsons, boarded the packet boat which had been chartered for the express purpose of conveying the jury and judges to the site of the burned tavern. If clear skies and sparkling sunlight presaged a good deliverance, she should not worry about her father's fate, thought Amity. But she was far from confident.

The daily boat was held back in order that the *George Washington* with its exclusive group of passengers might proceed on its course without the delays occasioned by the stops of a regular packet. With so august a body of legal officials aboard, Mr. James Sullivan did not wish to use his power as President of the Middlesex Canal Company to flaunt the rules which, as Attorney General, he was sworn to uphold. Everyone knew that passenger boats were forbidden to pass other packets on the canal to discourage racing and the subsequent washing out of the banks when boats went more than four miles an hour.

The October day was ablaze with color. Vivid reds and yellows were reflected in the canal's quiet waters, until the packet's bow shattered the mirrored surface and its bright hues into rippling gray.

But sun and breeze and gay foliage together could not give Amity the light heart such a day deserved. She sat silently beside Mlle. Armand, her nerves like taut wires. Would today's evidence impress the jurors with her father's innocence? Or would it convince them of his guilt?

She looked toward the other side of the vessel where the twelve men sat apart, their guard observing them through half-shut eyes. Could they know how deeply their decision would affect her life and future?

A quick step sounded behind her, and Sam strode into view. He had been appointed special assistant to his attorney cousin to demonstrate today's evidence.

"Would you ladies like an experienced guide to point out the sights?" His smile was too determined to be convincing.

Amity's effort to return it was as forced. "That would be very kind of you." Perhaps listening to Sam would take her mind off the terrible waiting.

"Just ahead is the famous aqueduct over the Mystic

River, borne by two stone abutments and three stone
piers. Each pier and abutment is twelve feet high, twenty
feet long, and about six feet in width. The surface of
the water in the aqueduct is ten feet above that of the
river at high tide." He stopped and shook a finger at her.
"Amity, you're not listening," he chided. "Don't you find
my store of information interesting?"

"It's very impressive," commented Mlle. Armand. Even
her usual serenity was marred by inward distress.

"Yes," echoed Amity, "it is impressive." But she could
not put any enthusiasm into the words. All she could
think of was her father's face, white and drawn as it had
been yesterday in the courtroom.

"I know that this waiting is hard for you, Amity."
Sam took her hands in his. "Just try to keep hoping.
Today's evidence is bound to help your father."

In the early forenoon the company debarked at the
site of the former tavern. Amity felt waves of revulsion
as she looked at the blackened timbers lying in a tangled
mass. Shards of earthen pots and twisted pieces of hard-
ware were scattered here and there. Loammi led the way
to the rear of the ruins, where the inn yard met the
marsh. Birds flitted about, tall grasses blew stiff and sere,
and cattails waved jagged tufts.

Loammi waited while the jurors ranged themselves
in a semicircle before him, their guard hovering close
by. To one side stood the justices and the Attorney
General. On the other side were Amity and Mlle. Armand.

The young lawyer raised his voice. "You have heard
that two months ago there occurred here an explosion
which resulted in the burning of this building. I propose

that the explosion was accidental—that marsh gas had collected underneath the inn, probably in the tightly confined space of the wine cellar, and that it was ignited by accident. We shall now observe a demonstration of the highly inflammable qualities of the natural gas that originates in this marsh."

Sam Baldwin stepped forward beside Loammi. He carried two round sticks about an inch in diameter and four feet long. He thrust them into the earth about three feet. Swiftly pulling one up, he held a lighted wisp of straw to the hole. There was a sharp pop and a momentary flash of fire. He pulled up the second stick, and as it emerged from the ground, held the brand to the hole. Again there was a sharp pop, and once more a brief blue flame.

The jurors watched intently. One cried out, "Say, young man, that's quite a trick. Can you do it again?"

Sam reached toward a heap of debris to pull up a wisp of dried grass to use as a torch. The tuft came up in his hand, revealing a small curved object half buried in the earth. Sam picked it up, peered at it intently, and gave a low whistle. Then he handed it to Loammi. "Here's another piece of evidence."

With his handkerchief Loammi carefully wiped mud from the piece of blackened clay. On his extended palm he displayed it.

"This, gentlemen of the jury, is the bowl of what was once Joe Beaver's pipe. You can clearly see the beaver incised upon it. Any number of Woburn citizens will testify that this belonged to the Indian in question. You are all witnesses to the fact that it was discovered on this spot a few scant minutes ago. I shall refer to this when we return to court."

The following day, while she waited for court to open, Amity's mind whirled back over the previous day's events. After dining at Warren's Tavern, the entire group had returned to Charlestown by the Middlesex Canal. The trip had seemed a slowly turning kaleidoscope of barges, bridges, locks, and finally the terminus.

Amity was keyed to a degree of tension she had not known possible. In an hour, perhaps less, she would know whether her father would be freed—or face an ig- nominious death.

In a daze she observed the opening of court. Nearly senseless with terror, she heard snatches of Loammi's peroration. ". . . that the chief witness could identify only the clothing and not the wearer . . . the hat and coat given to the Indian . . . his habit of smoking and his known appetite for liquor . . . the inflammable qualities of marsh gas . . . the presence of the unfortunate Indian's pipe probably broken in the explosion . . . that no one who has ten thousand dollars in Continental currency would be a Tory . . . that one of the witnesses was so uncertain of his testimony as to suggest perjury . . . that another witness of known honesty stated that Mr. Lyte was nearly half a mile away from the tavern at the time of the explosion . . . proving beyond a doubt the in- nocence of Darius Lyte."

Her eyes were riveted on the faces of the jurors as they listened to the Attorney General. Reviewing the evidence, he reminded the jury of the solemnity of the trial in establishing a proper estimate of human life.

Finally came Judge Parsons' charge to the jury. "These are the facts of the case," he concluded. "The duty of the court is now at an end and yours commences. The prisoner's life is in your keeping. Whether he shall be cut off from the land of the living and consigned to an ignominious death, or restored to liberty and his friends, depends on your present decision.

"If upon reviewing and duly considering the case you are satisfied that Darius Lyte is guilty, you must discharge your duty. But if you have well-founded and reasonable doubts as to his involvement in the case, you must acquit him. To you he has made his appeal, and to you hath the government given the power of deciding on his guilt or innocence. You will try the issue according to your evidence and according to your oath, and true deliverance make between the Commonwealth and the prisoner at the bar."

The jury filed out. Amity watched them go, her heart pounding. Her hands, clasped in her lap, were like ice, and wet with perspiration. A pain was shooting through her head, like a needle vibrating from temple to temple.

"Do you wish to go outside for a breath of air?" asked Mlle. Armand solicitously.

"Oh, no, I must be here when the jurors return."

"Sometimes they take a long time to deliberate," said Sam. Even his usually ruddy cheeks were pallid.

"I'll wait here," said Amity. She fixed her eye on a window at the far side of the room. A puff of cloud was in the lower corner. She watched it float slowly across the panes of glass, and out of sight. Another followed it. She counted six clouds passing across the window. As the seventh appeared, the door opened, and the jury returned.

If Amity's anxiety had been great before, it was as nothing compared to what it was at that moment. All of her being was concentrated in unbearable waiting. Her heart seemed to stop beating as she strained toward the moment when the decision would be announced.

She heard the foreman state that the jury was agreed. She waited breathlessly while her father was directed to hold up his right hand and look upon the jury. The jurors were ordered to look upon the prisoner.

The silence in the courtroom was stifling. Amity's ears were ringing.

"What is your verdict? Do you find the prisoner guilty or not guilty?" How awesomely solemn were the judge's questions.

Across the taut air of the courtroom came the foreman's words, clear and ringing. "We find him to be—not guilty!"

Not guilty! All the blood in Amity's body seemed to rush to her head. She thought it might burst from sheer relief. Her breathing seemed to have stopped. She could not move a muscle. She could only sit immobile, while her mind repeated the miraculous, the exquisitely beautiful words. Not guilty. Not guilty. Was ever a phrase more glorious?

Loammi had risen and was saying something, but she did not hear him. The judge spoke, but even his words could not penetrate the tumultuous "not guilty" resounding in her ears.

Then Loammi came toward her and spoke directly to

her, a smile lighting his face. All at once her self-control
gave way, and she had to fight desperately to keep from
weeping with joy as he said, "Your father has been
discharged to go without delay. I think you may all return to Woburn by the afternoon packet."

28

A New Life

The Darius Lyte who returned to the Rowan Tree Inn was thinner and paler than the man who had left it under duress two months before. A deep inner change was even more evident. Amity had not been mistaken when she thought at his arraignment that her father's eyes had lost their brooding expression of the past three years. During the period between his arrest and trial he had undergone a striking change.

On the day following his acquittal, Darius dressed with care and announced that he was going to call on Colonel Baldwin. Some of Amity's amazement must have shown in her face, for he said gently, "I don't wonder that you are surprised. During the days and nights in prison I took a long look at my past behavior and found it a deplorable waste. From now on I shall make the most of whatever time is left to me. First of all I want to thank Colonel Baldwin and beg his forgiveness for my selfishness and stupidity all these years."

Then he bent and kissed Amity's cheek. "And how

can I forgive myself for letting you carry the burdens that were rightfully mine?"

With a lightened heart she watched him go down the road toward the bridge over the canal. The air was clear, sunlight shone on brilliant foliage and sparkled on the water. And wonder of wonders, Darius Lyte was humming a tune as he strode down the road.

In the bright morning light the trial and its preceding weeks of anguish seemed like a dream. Yesterday on the homeward journey she had fitted together the puzzling events that had preceded her father's arrest.

Long ago Benjamin Thompson had planted the first seeds of distrust when he told Jedediah Rapp that Darius Lyte was a traitor. Naturally he would try to deflect suspicion from himself by laying the blame for the stolen information on the man who had refused to join him in betraying his own country. Ben Thompson had a reputation for using any person to further his own ends.

Those seeds of distrust had grown in the heat of inflamed passions during the Revolution, and had first flowered in the movement of the mob against the young Darius Lyte. They had kept the malice alive during his absence, and had blossomed again upon his return. Doubtless, Strobo Dix knew of the feeling against Darius, and had felt safe in voicing his suspicion that Darius had set off the explosion. No wonder Jedediah Rapp, giddy with hatred and strong drink, had led the mob against the Rowan Tree Inn. No wonder he had mistaken Joe Beaver, clothed as he was, for Darius.

Poor Joe Beaver. Amity's heart contracted in pity. He had probably slept for a time near the tavern, then lighted his pipe and made his way into the cellar for a drink. The moment he opened the door of the wine cellar, a spark from his pipe must have ignited the pent-up gas that had risen from the marsh through the dirt floor and filled the confined space of the compartment. The explosion must have blown the bowl of his pipe up and out into the yard with other debris, and it had lain there until Sam pulled aside the tuft of grass.

What a horrible way for the old Indian to die! Though the end must have come so quickly that Joe could not have known what happened, she could not help a strong feeling of sympathy. Then she recalled his words—"Joe Beaver go to Great Father soon." He had not exhibited any fear then. Perhaps he was thankful to have his earthly problems ended.

As for Strobo Dix and Luke Fenwick, they had announced immediately after the trial their decision to leave the district. They had heard that a new inland waterway would be built in New York State. The proposed Erie Canal would be longer and more prosperous than the Middlesex. They would buy land there and build another tavern with the insurance money from their unfortunate venture in Woburn.

Slowly Amity made her way through the house, letting her fingers touch a polished table, then a gleaming sconce. An idea had been growing in her mind for some time. Today she would speak to Aunt Keziah.

She found her aunt sitting in the courtyard in a sunny sheltered spot. A host of birds trilled and warbled—cedar waxwings, goldfinches, myrtle warblers. High in a lofty perch a downy woodpecker drummed.

"Aunt Keziah," began Amity, dropping onto a stool at the elderly woman's side, "there's something I'd like to discuss with you."

"Yes, my dear?" The dame folded her veined hands and regarded Amity with eyes that were happy and serene.

"I've been thinking about Father," said Amity. "It doesn't seem right for him not to have title to this house —someday." How difficult to talk about wills and inheritances with the person most involved, almost like discussing her death.

"You are the one who should own the property. It was your courage that kept it for us." Aunt Keziah's voice was firm.

"I would love it to be mine eventually, but I'd rather Father owned it first. I think he will remain here now. And when he no longer needs it, then it can come to me. And then to Tim. Couldn't you make some arrangement like that, Aunt Keziah?"

"If you wish it that way, my dear, I imagine that young Loammi can draw up papers to ensure such a disposition." Her hand sought Amity's and patted it.

That day and the day after, Amity moved in a glow of gratitude. The sound of her father's boots upon the stairs, the sight of his lean figure, the murmur of his voice—each sent a wave of thankfulness through her. How close he had come to death she dared not think. That he was free and safely home once more was enough.

She was well aware that Darius spent more and more time in Mlle. Armand's company. Who would not enjoy being with the fascinating Frenchwoman? Her loyalty was deep and sincere. Amity was certain she could not have survived the weeks of anxiety without her warm, sustaining friendship.

One evening after the few guests had gone to their rooms, Mlle. Armand, Darius, and Amity sat together in the parlor, the Frenchwoman in a rose velvet chair, her mauve gown shimmering in the candlelight.

"Now that your family is so happily reunited, there is no reason for me to remain here, pleasant though it is. I have made plans to leave at the end of this week."

"Leave?" asked Darius. He rose and walked toward her, his face troubled.

With a new poignancy Amity realized how much Mlle. Armand meant to her. "Must you go back to Hartford?" she asked. "Surely Mr. Pratt can find another governess —although never one like you!"

The ghost of a smile played about Mlle. Armand's lips. "During the summer Mr. Pratt decided that he had more need of a wife than a governess, although it is possible that he once may have wished me to combine the roles." She smoothed the lace at her cuff. "Since I have been here, he has engaged another governess," she said, "and has asked me to return to be his wife."

Darius Lyte stepped back a pace. He cleared his throat. "Mr. Pratt is an important man in Connecticut, I understand."

"Yes, very important. He is well educated, intelligent, and of considerable financial solidity," said Mlle. Armand.

"Then I suppose we can only offer you our felicitations," said Darius. Was Amity fancying it, or had the old glower returned to his face?

"I hope you will be very happy," said Amity. Her voice faltered, and she was near to tears. After Mlle. Armand was married, nothing would be the same. There would be no more visits, no more tender confidences.

"Do not be in such a hurry," chided Mlle. Armand. "I did not say that I had accepted his proposal. On the contrary, I have decided that marriage, no matter how advantageous from a material standpoint, is not possible for me without love. No, I shall not go to Hartford. Instead I shall book passage on the next available vessel for Charleston, South Carolina. My brother has a plantation there. He is lonely, and needs someone. It is good to be needed." She lowered her eyes.

Darius Lyte bent over the Frenchwoman and put one long-fingered hand beneath her chin. "Do you think that your brother is the only one who needs you?" he asked, tilting her face upward. "Have you any inkling how much your presence here has meant to all of us—to me especially? Whose face did I dream of in the long prison nights? Whose voice did I long to hear?" He took her hands in his and drew her to her feet. "Whose but yours, my dear Cécile?"

Amity rose and started to tiptoe from the room. She could have stamped with all her might. They would never have heard her. She had reached the threshold when her father spoke again. "Do you think your lonely brother could be persuaded to accept a painted likeness in lieu of yourself? I have longed to do a portrait of you since you first came to this house. In that chair would be perfect, with the blue drapery at one side."

"Oho! So it is a model you wish." There was a teasing

note in the Frenchwoman's voice. "You men are all alike. Mr. Pratt wanted a governess, and you—"

"I am not looking for a model, Cécile. Could you, would you consent to become—"

Amity did not hear the rest of the sentence. Her feet carried her swiftly away and out of earshot. She had never felt so unnecessary before. Nor so completely happy. If she herself had sought someone to play a mother's role, she could not have found anyone more to her liking than the tender yet strong Frenchwoman. What a blessing for all the Lytes if she would remain here!

Her father's words struck her with a new impact. A portrait of Mlle. Armand! Surely she had heard him correctly. He had said he wanted to paint her portrait! All at once she was filled with bubbling joy. Her father would once more be a limner, and would use the talent and skill he had worked to perfect. She could have danced for delight.

Longing to tell someone, she went to Nicole's room and peeped in, then to Bessie's, and even her aunt's. But each occupant was sleeping soundly. She went to her own room and hopefully peered out the window. Perhaps Sam or even Loammi was in Woburn and might be out walking this evening. She needed someone with whom to share this glorious news.

But towpath and road were empty and silent, and the Baldwin mansion dark. Vaguely dejected, Amity left the window and prepared for bed.

The next morning in the midst of felicitations and congratulations to Mlle. Armand and Darius Lyte, Tim wondered aloud if Sam and Loammi would be able to attend the wedding. Or would they be on their way to Europe?

Sam—going to Europe? Amity spun around. "Where did you hear that?" she demanded of her brother.

"Oh, I thought you knew about it. George says Loam-mi is going to study canals and tunnels and things like that in Europe, and he wants Sam to go with him."

Why hadn't Sam told her? Amity hated hearing things secondhand. Then she realized that nearly a week had passed since she had seen Sam. Possibly the plans had been made after the trial. And during that time she had been absorbed in her father's plight to the exclusion of all else.

She could imagine how pleased Sam was at the prospect. Nothing was so fascinating to him as the study of construction. And if there was one person in the world he admired more than his uncle, it was his cousin, Loammi. She recalled Loammi's words the night of the ball, his wish to leave the practice of law and enter into the new science of civil engineering. He would be a pioneer in the field, and Sam would work with him, lending his keen mind and unbounded vitality.

But though she was glad for Sam, Amity could not subdue a gnawing unhappiness. Sam might have given her some warning, some hint that he was going away. She couldn't help feeling a twinge of envy. How she wished she might venture into new fields, too. And the prospect of Sam's absence for months, perhaps years, filled her with desolation.

There was no point in mooning over it, though. She knew a remedy for low spirits. Hadn't she learned in the past dreary weeks that work brought relief?

Tomorrow was wash day. She would change the linen on all the beds. She climbed the stairs, fighting an impulse to look down the road to the Baldwin house.

In the upper hallway she found Nance bundling sheets and towels into one vast armload. And in her bedroom was Nicole, smoothing a snowy spread over the four-poster. "You're too late," she said brightly to Amity. "I'm just finishing."

Downstairs Amity approached Bessie. "What can I do to help you?" she asked the cook.

Bessie set a handful of forks in the rack. "There are rolls to shape," she said, "but Nicole has a new way of twisting them." She paused uncertainly.

"You'd like Nicole to make them. I know," said Amity. "Is there anything else?"

"Chickens to stuff," said Bessie, "but I'm trying out a new dressing. I guess I don't need any help right now."

Surely there was something in this sprawling house that required her attention. Or outside. Amity walked briskly to the courtyard where Bill Trask was raking the leaves up from the lawn.

"Would you like a helper?" asked Amity eagerly.

He regarded her doubtfully. "Can't say as I do. I'm just finishing up this patch of leaves, and then I'm going to spread some cow droppings—no work for a lady."

Amity put up her chin determinedly. Just because everything was running smoothly was no reason for her to feel superfluous. She marched toward the front of the house. Surely she could offer some assistance with the accounts.

In the parlor Mlle. Armand and Darius Lyte sat close

together at the desk. She had a pen in her hand, and was saying, "But of course I will continue to do the accounts. It is the business of the wife to aid the husband. It will give me something to do while you are busy with limning."

Amity went by the door without a word. There was no point in even offering help. She heard her father saying, "I must send for oils today. With luck they should arrive within the week, and I can begin your portrait."

Even Aunt Keziah was occupied. When Amity wandered into the sitting room, she found her writing a letter.

"Is there anything I can do to help you?"

The dame looked up with an air of distraction. Her eyes flicked toward the window, and she said, "I'd like it well were you to chase that cat away. The plaguey creature is after my birds again."

Listlessly Amity went out the door. She clapped her hands at the cat and ran at it halfheartedly. The animal seemed to sense her indifference, and took a stance, glaring at her. Not until she picked up a handful of acorns and threw them in its direction did it turn and cross the lawn.

Something about its retreat was not convincing. Amity followed it across the road and to the towpath, and watched it walk sedately out of sight, its orange and white tail waving.

Hoofs sounded on the path, and a horse came into view, straining against its harness, the towrope stretching to the barge behind. The driver switched a twig across the beast's shoulders and smiled a toothy grin.

"A great day, Miss," he said, twisting around on his saddle to watch her as he passed by.

"It is indeed," she answered. In her ears the words sounded spiritless. What was the matter with her? The day was beautiful, with great puffs of cloud sailing majestically in a sky of deepest blue. She was well and healthy; her father was free; he would soon take as his wife a wise and charming woman; and he was resuming portrait painting. She had everything to be thankful for, and yet she was feeling as sour as the wizened green apples scattered across the path.

The barge floated by, its decks covered with hogsheads of pearlash and potash for the soap factories in Boston. On the rear deck a woman scrubbed at a tub of laundry, suds billowing over the sides. She lifted a dripping fist and pushed a lock of hair from her eyes. The steersman yelled cheerfully, "How about a cuppa coffee, Meg? I've got a hungry feeling."

The woman wiped her hands on her half-soaked apron. "These duds'll wait. I'll put the pot on." She turned, waved a broad arm at Amity, and said in a confiding tone, "Got to keep these men fed and happy," and walked into the tiny shelter.

Amity sat down on a log beside the towpath. Why did she feel more unhappy than ever? Just seeing the man and woman together gave her a sense of unbearable loneliness.

The forked wake of the barge widened until the prongs lost themselves in the banks. The surface of the water slowly quieted. Gradually it took on the smoothness of a mirror. Amity could see the sky and clouds reflected, and on the opposite side the trees. She could even make out a pale lavender blur that was herself. She leaned forward to get a better look. Out of the corner of her eye she saw a russet shape striding into the glasslike scene.

Surely it was a mirage! That couldn't be Sam. He was somewhere in Cambridge or Boston with Loammi, making preparations for their trip. Perhaps if she shut her eyes for a moment and then opened them, the picture would be as it had been before, with just one lavender figure on the bank. She let her eyelids drop. When they flew up the russet was still there. She turned her head, and saw Sam hurrying toward her, his face bright with eagerness.

"Oughtn't you to be packing for your trip?" she asked testily.

He chuckled, and sat beside her on the log. "Are you in such a hurry to get rid of me? Loammi is leaving tomorrow, but I shan't go for a month. I've some things to attend to before joining him in England."

A month was better than nothing, but she couldn't stifle a pang at the prospect of the loneliness ahead.

He looked into her face. "Is something troubling you? I'd thought to find you happy as a lark—your father exonerated, and the inn prospering."

She kicked at a pebble. "The inn!" she sniffed. "I wish I'd never thought of the idea!"

He looked at her incredulously. "But you told me you loved the house, that you thought it was perfect!"

"It's just that it's so big," she said in confusion, "and so full of people—" She broke off to stare moodily at the water.

"You could bear to leave it—say in a month's time?"

252 / the limner's daughter

Something in his voice caught at her. She looked at him in question.

"I've decided to go into civil engineering," he continued, "building some of the bridges, tunnels, and highways this country needs. And of course canals. It's a new field and untried. I may never be successful, but it's what I must do."

He rose, took her hands in his firm grasp, and drew her to her feet. "Would you have the courage to share such a life, Amity?"

Her mind flew back over the past year and a half. Who had steadied and cheered her on the Connecticut mudflats? Who had found her in Boston when the future looked so bleak? Who had led the canal crew to scatter the attacking mob? And who had stood stanchly by during the dark days of her father's trial?

Sam. It had always been Sam, whenever she needed a champion. Happiness shot through her. She had never been so sure of a decision in her life.

Her heart in her eyes, she gave him her answer.

ACKNOWLEDGMENTS

For the generous sharing of his collected material about the Middlesex Canal, my thanks are due to Prescott W. Hall, President of the Salem, N.H., Historical Society.

In the reconstruction of a trial as it might have taken place in 1806, I am indebted to Dr. Edith G. Henderson, Curator of the Treasure Room of the Harvard Law Library, who furnished historical data and shared her specialized skills in checking the trial scenes in manuscript.

I am also grateful for the privilege of using the Baldwin manuscripts and related materials at the Houghton Library, Harvard University, and for the kind assistance given at the Middlesex Law Library Association, the Woburn and the Melrose Public Libraries, and the Bostonian Society.

ABOUT THE AUTHOR

Writing historical novels is a dream come true for Mary Stetson Clarke. As a girl she was fascinated by the past, and today her re-creations of life in other days are transporting present-day readers to early periods in American history. The vitality and authenticity which characterize her books are based on painstaking historical research.

Mrs. Clarke was born and brought up in Melrose, Massachusetts, attended public schools there, and went on to Boston University and Columbia. She worked on *The Christian Science Monitor* and at Harvard University, and studied and later taught creative writing at the Boston Center for Adult Education. Except for a few years in the New York area, she has lived in Melrose, where she takes an active part in community affairs.

After her marriage to Edwin L. Clarke, an electrical engineer, and the birth of their son and two daughters, Mrs. Clarke contributed many feature articles to various newspapers and magazines. While her children were in their teens she began writing historical novels, and now that her family is grown, she continues to write for young people, sharing with them her lively enthusiasm for our country in its early days.